H. C. Bailey

Mr. Fortune's Practice

e-artnow 2022

H. C. Bailey
Mr. Fortune's Practice

e-artnow, 2022
Contact: info@e-artnow.org

ISBN 978-80-273-4352-2

Contents

THE ASCOT TRAGEDY	12
THE PRESIDENT OF SAN JACINTO	24
THE YOUNG DOCTOR	36
THE MAGIC STONE	49
THE SNOWBALL BURGLARY	60
THE LEADING LADY	70
THE UNKNOWN MURDERER	82

CASE I

THE ASCOT TRAGEDY

THAT is what it would have been called in the evening papers if they had known all about it. They did not. They made the most of the mystery, you remember; it was not good for them or you to know that the sequel was a sequel. But there is no reason why the flats should not be joined now.

So let us begin at Ascot on the morning of that Cup Day. One of our fine summers, the course rather yellow, the lawns rather brown, a haze of heat over the distant woodland, and sunshine flaming about the flounces and silk hats. There were already many of both in the Royal Enclosure (it was a year of flounces), and among them, dapper, debonair, everybody's friend, the youngest middle-aged man in Europe. He, of course, is the Hon. Sidney Lomas, the Chief of the Criminal Investigation Department, though mistaken by some outsiders for a comic actor of fame. Tripping back from a joke with the stewards, he discovered, sprawling solitary on the end of one of the seats, Mr. Fortune, the adviser of him and all other official and important people when surgery, medicine or kindred sciences can elucidate what is or is not crime. No one looks more prosperous than Reginald Fortune. He is plump and pinkly healthy, he and his tailor treat each other with respect, his countenance has the amiability of a nice boy.

But on this occasion Lomas found fault with him. "Why, Fortune, you're very pensive. Have you lost the lady of your present affections? Or backed a wrong 'un?"

"Go away. No fellow has a right to be as cool as you look. Go quite away. I feel like the three fellows in the Bible who sang in the furnace. How can you jest, Lomas? I have no affections. I cannot love, to bet I am ashamed. I always win. Half-crowns. Why is the world thus, Lomas?"

"My dear fellow, you're not yourself. You look quite professional."

Reggie Fortune groaned. "I am. This place worries me. I am anatomical, ethnological, anthropological."

"Good Gad," said Lomas.

"Yes. A distressing place, look at it"; he waved a stick.

The people in the Royal Enclosure were as pleasant to behold as usual. Comely girls and women who had been comely passed in frocks of which many were pretty and few garish; their men were of a blameless, inconspicuous uniformity.

"What is he?" said Reggie Fortune. "I ask you. Look at his feet."

What Lomas saw was a man dressed like all the rest of them and as well set up, but of a darker complexion. He did not see anything remarkable. "The big fellow?" he said. "He is a little weak at the knee. But what's the matter with him?"

"Who is he?" said Reggie Fortune.

Lomas shrugged. "Not English, of course. Rather a half-caste colour, isn't he? From one of the smaller legations, I suppose, Balkan or South American." He waved a hand to some elegant aliens who were at that moment kissing ladies' hands with florid grace. "They all come here, you know."

"I don't know," said Reggie Fortune peevishly. "Half-caste? Half what caste? Look at his feet." Now the man's feet, well displayed beneath white spats, were large and flat but distinguished by their heels, which stuck out behind extravagantly. "That is the negro heel."

"My dear Fortune! The fellow is no more a negro than I am," Lomas protested: and indeed the man's hair was straight and sleek and he had a good enough nose, and he was far from black.

"The negro or Hamitic heel," Reggie Fortune drowsily persisted. "I suspect the Hamitic or negro leg. And otherwise up above. And it's all very distressing, Lomas."

"An Egyptian or perhaps an Arab: probably a Foreign Office pet," Lomas consoled him. "That would get him into the Royal Enclosure."

Lomas was then removed by a duchess and Reggie Fortune tilted his hat still farther over his eyes and pondered whether it would be wise to drink before lunch and was dreamily aware of other people on his seat, an old man darkly tanned and soldierly in the custody of a little woman brilliantly dressed and terribly vivacious. She chattered without a pause, she made eyes, she made affectionate movements and little caresses. The old man though helpless seemed to be thinking of something else. And Reggie Fortune sketched lower and still lower estimates of human nature.

They went away at last when everybody went away to gather in a crowd at the gates and along the railings for the coming of the King. You will please to observe that the time must have been about one o'clock.

Reggie Fortune, one of the few, remained on his seat. He heard the cheering down the course and had sufficient presence of mind to stand up and take off his hat as the distant band began to play. Over the heads of the crowd he saw the red coats of the postilions and a gleam of the grey of the team as the King's carriage swept round into the enclosure. The rest of the procession passed and the crowd melted away. But one man remained by the railings alone. He was tall and thin and he leaned limply against the railings, one arm hanging over them. After a little while he turned on his heel and fell in a heap.

Two of the green-coated wardens of the gate ran up to him. "Oh, Lord," Reggie Fortune groaned, "why did I be a doctor?" But before he could get through the flurry of people the man was being carried away.

The gift of Lomas for arriving where he wants to be displayed itself. Lomas slid through the crowd and took his arm, "Stout fellow! Come along. It's Sir Arthur Dean. Touch of sun, what?"

"Arthur Dean? That's the Persia man, pundit on the Middle East?"

"That's the fellow. Getting old, you know. One of the best."

Into the room where the old man lay came the shouting over the first race. By the door Lomas and an inspector of police talked in low tones, glancing now and then at Reggie, who was busy.

"Merry Man! Merry Man! Merry Man!" the crowd roared outside.

Reggie straightened his bent back and stood looking down at his patient. Lomas came forward. "Anything we can get you, Fortune? Would you like some assistance?"

"You can't assist him," said Reggie. "He's dead."

"Merry Man!" the crowd triumphed. "Merry Man!"

"Good Gad!" said Lomas. "Poor fellow. One of the best. Well, well, what is it? Heart failure?"

"The heart generally fails when you die," Reggie mumbled: he still stared down at the body and the wonted benignity of his face was lost in expressionless reserve. "Do you know if he has any people down here?"

"It's possible. There is a married son. I'll have him looked for." Lomas sent his inspector off.

"I saw the old man with a woman just before he died," Reggie murmured, and Lomas put up his eyeglass.

"Did you though? Very sudden, wasn't it? And he was all alone when he died."

"When he fell," Reggie mumbled the correction. "Yes, highly sudden."

"What was the cause of death, Fortune?"

"I wonder," Reggie muttered. He went down on his knees by the body, he looked long and closely into the eyes, he opened the clothes... and to the eyes he came back again. Then there was a tap at the door and Lomas having conferred there came back and said, "The son and his wife. I'll tell them. I suppose they can see the body?"

"They'd better see the body," said Reggie, and as Lomas went out he began to cover and arrange it. He was laying the right arm by the side when he checked and held it up to the light. On the back of the hand was a tiny drop of blood and a red smear. He looked close and found such a hole as a pin might make.

From the room outside came a woman's cry, then a deep man's voice in some agitation, and Lomas opened the door. "This is Mr. Fortune, the surgeon who was with your father at once. Major Dean and Mrs. Dean, Fortune."

Reggie bowed and studied them. The man was a soldierly fellow, with his father's keen, wary face. But it was the woman Reggie watched, the woman who was saying, "I was with him only half an hour ago," and twisting her hands nervously.

"Most of that half-hour he has been dead. Where did you leave him, madam?" Reggie said.

Husband and wife stared at him. "Why, in the Royal Enclosure, of course. In the crowd when the King came. I—I lost him. Somebody spoke to me. Yes, it was Sybil. And I never saw him again."

Reggie stepped aside from the body. She shuddered and hid her face in her hands. "His eyes-his eyes," she murmured.

Major Dean blew his nose. "This rather knocks one over," he said. "What's the cause of death, sir?"

"Can you help me?" said Reggie.

"I? What do you mean?"

"Nothing wrong with his heart, was there?"

"Never heard of it. He didn't use doctors. Never was ill."

Reggie stroked his chin. "I suppose he hadn't been to an oculist lately?"

"Not he. His eyes were as good as mine. Wonderful good. He used to brag of it. He was rising seventy and no glasses. Good Lord, what's that got to do with it? I want to know why he died."

"So do I. And I can't tell you," said Reggie.

"What? I say-what? You mean a post-mortem. That's horrible."

"My dear Major, it is most distressing," Lomas purred. "I assure you anything in our power-sympathize with your feelings, quite, quite. But the Coroner would insist, you know; we have no choice."

"As you were saying," Reggie chimed in, "we want to know why he died."

Major Dean drew a long breath. "That's all right, that's all right," he said. "The old dad!" and he came to his father's side and knelt down, and his wife stood by him, her hand on his shoulder. He looked a moment into the dead face, and closed the eyes and looked long.

From this scene Reggie and Lomas drew back. In the silence they heard the man and woman breathing unsteadily. Lomas sighed his sympathy. Mrs. Dean whispered, "His mouth! Oh, Claude, his mouth!" and with a sudden darting movement wiped away some froth from the pale lips. Then she too knelt and she kissed the brow. Her husband lifted the dead right hand to hold it for a while. And then he reached across to the key chain, took off the keys, slipped them into his pocket and helped his wife to her feet.

Reggie turned a still expressionless face on Lomas. Lomas still exhibited grave official sorrow.

"Well-er-thanks very much for all you've done," Major Dean addressed them both. "You've been very kind. We feel that. And if you will let me know as soon as you know anything-rather a relief."

"Quite, quite." Lomas held out his hand; Major Dean took it. "Yes, I'm so sorry, but you see we must take charge of everything for the present." He let the Major's hand go and still held out his own.

Dean flushed. "What, his keys?"

"Thank you," said Lomas, and at last received them.

"I was thinking about his papers, you know."

"I can promise you they'll be safe."

"Oh, well, that settles it!" Dean laughed. "You know where to find me," and he took his wife, who was plainly eager to speak to him, away.

Lomas dandled the keys in his hand. "I wonder what's in their minds? And what's in yours, Fortune?"

"Man was murdered," said Reggie.

Lomas groaned, "I was afraid you had that for me. But surely it's not possible?"

"It ought not to be," Reggie admitted. "At a quarter to one he was quite alive, rather bored perhaps, but as fit as me. At a quarter past he was dead. What happened in between?"

"Why, he was in sight the whole time — —"

"All among the most respectable people in England. Yet he dies suddenly of asphyxia and heart failure. Why?"

"Well, some obscure heart trouble — —" Lomas protested.

"He was in the pink. He never used doctors. You heard them say so. He hadn't even been to an oculist."

"A fellow doesn't always know," Lomas urged. "There are all sorts of heart weakness."

"Not this sort." Reggie shook his head. "And the eyes. Did you see how those two were afraid of his eyes? Your eyes won't look like that when you die of heart failure. They might if an oculist had put belladonna in 'em to examine you. But there was no oculist. Dilated pupils, foam at the mouth, cold flesh. He was poisoned. It might have been aconitine. But aconitine don't kill so quick or quite so quiet."

"What is aconitine?"

"Oh, wolf-bane. Blue-rocket. You can get it from other plants. Only this is too quick. It slew him like prussic acid and much more peacefully. Some alkaloid poison of the aconite family, possibly unclassified. Probably it was put into him by that fresh puncture in his hand while he was packed in the crowd, just a scratch, just a jab with a hollow needle. An easy murder if you could trust your stuff. And when we do the post-mortem we'll find that everything points to death by a poison we can't trace."

"Thanks, so much," said Lomas. "It is for this we employ experts."

"Well, the police also must earn their bread. Who is he?"

"He was the great authority on the Middle East. Old Indian civilian long retired. Lately political adviser to the Government of Media. You know all that."

"Yes. Who wanted him dead?" said Reggie.

"Oh, my dear fellow!" Lomas spread out his hands. "The world is wide."

"Yes. The world also is very evil. The time also is waxing late. Same like the hymn says. What about those papers son and co. were so keen on?"

Lomas laughed. "If you could believe I have a little intelligence, it would so soothe me. Our people have been warned to take charge of his flat."

"Active fellow. Let's go and see what they found."

It was not much more than an hour before a policeman was letting them into Sir Arthur Dean's flat in Westminster. An inspector of police led the way to the study. "Anything of interest, Morton?" Lomas said.

"Well, sir, nothing you could call out of the way. When we came, the servants had heard of the death and they were upset. Sir Arthur's man, he opened the door to me fairly crying. Been with him thirty years, fine old-fashioned fellow, would be talking about his master."

Lomas and Reggie looked at each other, but the inspector swept on.

"Then in this room, sir, there was Sir Arthur's executor, Colonel Osbert, getting out papers. I had to tell him that wouldn't do. Rather stiff he was. He is a military man. Well, sir, I put it to him, orders are orders, and he took it very well. But he let me see pretty plain he didn't like it. He was quite the gentleman, but he put it to me we had no business in Sir Arthur's affairs unless we thought there was foul play. Well, of course, I couldn't answer that. He talked a good deal, fishing, you might say. All he got out of me was that I couldn't allow anything to be touched. So he said he would take it up with the Commissioner and went off. That's all, sir."

"Who is he?" said Reggie.

"His card, sir. Colonel Osbert, late Indian Army."

"Do you know if he was who he said he was?" Lomas asked.

The inspector was startled. "Well, sir, the servants knew him. Sir Arthur's man, he let him in, says he's Sir Arthur's oldest friend. I had no reason to detain him."

"That's all right, Morton," said Lomas. "Well, what time did you get here?"

"Your message came two o'clock, sir. I should say we were here by a quarter past."

Lomas nodded and dismissed him. "Quick work," he said with a cock of his eye at Reggie.

"We can time it all by the King. He drove up the course at ten past one. Till the procession came Sir Arthur was alive. We didn't pick him up till five minutes after, at the least. No one knew he was dead till you had examined him. No one knew then but me and my men. And yet Colonel Osbert in London knows of the death in time to get round here and get to work on the dead man's papers before two-fifteen. He knew the man was dead as soon as we did who were looking at the body. Damme, he has very early information."

"Yes. One to you, Lomas. And a nasty one for Colonel Osbert. Our active and intelligent police force. If you hadn't been up and doing and sent your bright boys round, Colonel Osbert might have got away with what he wanted. And he wouldn't have had to explain how he knew too much."

"When was the poison given? Say between five to one and ten past. At that time the murderer was in the Royal Enclosure. If he had his car waiting handy, could he get here before two-fifteen?"

"Well-if his car was a flier, and there were no flies on his chauffeur and he had luck all the way, I suppose it's possible. But I don't believe in it. I should say Osbert didn't do the job."

Lomas sprang up and called the inspector. He wanted to know what Colonel Osbert was wearing. Colonel Osbert was in a lounge suit of grey flannel. Lomas sat down again and lit a cigarette. "I'm afraid that will do for an alibi, Fortune," he sighed. "Your hypothetical murderer was in the Royal Enclosure. Therefore——"

"He was in topper and tails, same like us. The uniform of respectability. Of course, he could have done a change in his car. But I don't think it. No. Osbert won't do. But what was he after?"

Lomas stood up and looked round the room. It had the ordinary furniture of an old-fashioned study and in addition several modern steel chests of drawers for filing documents. "Well, he set some value on his papers," Lomas said.

"Lots of honest toil before you, Lomas, old thing." Reggie smiled, and while Lomas fell to work with the keys he wandered about picking up a bowl here, a brass tray there. "He kept to his own line," he remarked. "Everything is Asiatic."

"You may well say so," Lomas groaned, frowning over a mass of papers.

But Reggie's attention was diverted. Somebody had rung the bell and there was talk in the hall. He made out a woman's voice. "I fancy this is our young friend the daughter-in-law," he murmured.

Lomas looked up at him. "I had a notion you didn't take to her, Fortune. Do you want to see her?"

"God forbid," said Reggie. "She's thin, Lomas, she's too thin."

In a moment or two a discreet tap introduced Inspector Morton. "Mrs. Dean, deceased's daughter-in-law, sir," he reported. "Asked to see the man-servant. I saw no objection, me being present. They were both much distressed, sir. She asked him if Colonel Osbert had been here. Seemed upset when she heard he was here before us. Asked if he had taken anything away. The servant told her we weren't letting anything be touched. That didn't seem to satisfy her. She said something nasty about the police being always too late. Meant for me, I suppose."

"I rather fancy it was meant for me," said Reggie. "It's a bad business."

"I don't think the Colonel got away with anything, sir. He was sitting down to the diary on the table there when we came in."

"All right." Lomas waved him away. "Damme, it is a bad business. What am I to do with this, Fortune?" He held up papers in a strange script, papers of all sorts and sizes, some torn and discoloured, some fresh.

Reggie went to look. "Arabic," he said. "And this is Persian." He studied them for a while. "A sort of dossier, a lot of evidence about some case or person. Lomas old thing, you'll have to call in the Foreign Office."

"Lord, we can translate them ourselves. It's the mass of it!"

"Yes, lot of light reading. I think I should have a talk to the Foreign Office. Well, that's your show. Me for the body."

Lomas lay back in his chair. "What's in your head?"

"I won't let anything into my head. There is no evidence. But I'm wondering if we'll ever get any. It's a beautiful crime-as a crime. A wicked world, Lomas old thing."

On the day after, Reggie Fortune came into Lomas's room at Scotland Yard and shook his head and lit one of Lomas's largest cigars and fell into a chair. "Unsatisfactory, highly unsatisfactory," he announced. "I took Harvey down with me. You couldn't have a better opinion except mine, and he agrees with me."

"And what do you say?"

"I say, nothing doing. He had no medical history. There was nothing the matter with the man, yet he died of heart failure and suffocation. That means poisoning by aconitine or a similar alkaloid. But there is no poison in the price list which would in a quarter of an hour kill quietly and without fuss a man in perfect health. I have no doubt a poison was injected into him by that puncture on the hand, but I don't know what it was. We'll have some analysis done, of course, but I expect nothing of that. There'll be no trace."

"Unique case."

"I wouldn't say that. You remember I thought General Blaker was poisoned. He was mixed up with Asiatics too. There were queer circumstances about the death of that Greek millionaire in Rome two years ago. The world's old and men have been poisoning each other for five thousand years and science only began to look into it yesterday. There's a lot of drugs in the world that you can't buy at the chemist's."

"Good Gad," Lomas protested, "we're in Scotland Yard, not the Arabian Nights. What you mean is you can't do anything?"

"Even so. Can you? Who wanted him dead?"

"Nobody but a lunatic. He had no money to leave. He was on the best terms with his son. He was a popular old boy, never had an enemy. He had no secrets-most respectable-lived all his life in public."

"And yet his son snatched at his keys before he was cold. And his dear old friend Osbert knew of his death before he was dead and made a bee-line for his papers. By the way, what was in his papers?"

Lomas shrugged. "Our fellows are working at 'em."

"And who is Osbert?"

"Well, you know, he's coming to see me. He put in his protest to the Commissioner, and they were going to turn him down, of course. But I thought I'd like to listen to Colonel Osbert."

"Me too," said Reggie.

"By all means, my dear fellow. But he seems quite genuine. He is the executor. He is an old friend, about the oldest living. Not a spot on his record. Long Indian service."

"Only son and daughter don't seem to trust him. Only he also is a bit Asiatic."

"Oh, my dear Fortune ——" Lomas was protesting when Colonel Osbert came.

You will find a hundred men like him on any day in the service clubs. He was small and brown and neat, even dapper, but a trifle stiff in the joints. His manner of speech was a drawl concluding with a bark.

Reggie lay back in his chair and admired the bland fluency with which Lomas said nothing in reply to the parade-ground demands of Colonel Osbert. Colonel Osbert wanted to know (if we may reduce many sentences to one) what Lomas meant by refusing him possession of Sir Arthur Dean's papers. And Lomas continued to reply that he meant nothing in particular.

"Sudden death at Ascot-in the Royal Enclosure too," he explained. "That's very startling and conspicuous. The poor fellow hadn't been ill, as far as we can learn. Naturally we have to seek for any explanation."

So at last Osbert came out with: "What, sir, you don't mean to say, sir-suspect foul play?"

"Oh, my dear Colonel, you wouldn't suggest that?"

"I, sir? Never entered my head. Poor dear Arthur! A shock, sir. A blow! Getting old, of course, like the rest of us."

"Ah, had he been failing?" said Reggie sympathetically.

"Well, well, well. We none of us grow younger, sir." Colonel Osbert shook his head. "But upon my soul, Mr. Lomas, I don't understand the action of your department."

"I'm so sorry you should say that," Lomas sighed. "Now I wonder if you have particular reason for wanting Sir Arthur's papers at once?"

"My good sir, I am his executor. It's my duty to take charge of his papers."

"Quite, quite. Well, they're all safe, you know. His death must have been a great shock to you, Colonel."

"Shock, sir? A blow, a blow. Poor dear Arthur!"

"Yes, too bad," Lomas mourned: and voice and face were all kindly innocence as he babbled on: "I suppose you heard about it from his son?"

Colonel Osbert paused to clear his throat. Colonel Osbert stopped that one. "Major Dean? No, sir. No. Point of fact, I don't know who the fellow was. Some fellow called me up on the 'phone and told me poor dear Arthur had fallen down dead on the course. Upon my soul, I was knocked over, absolutely knocked over. When I came to myself I rushed round to secure his papers."

"Why, did you think somebody would be after them?"

"My dear sir!" Colonel Osbert protested. "Really, now really. It was my duty. Arthur was always very strict with his papers. I thought of his wishes."

"Quite, quite," Lomas purred, and artless as ever he went on: "Mrs. Dean was round at the flat too."

"God bless my soul!" said Colonel Osbert.

"I wonder if you could tell me: is there anyone who would have an interest in getting hold of his papers?"

Colonel Osbert again cleared his throat. "I can tell you this, sir. I don't understand the position of Mrs. Dean and her husband. And I shall be glad, I don't mind owning, I shall be very glad to have poor dear Arthur's papers in my hands."

"Ah, thank you so much," said Lomas, and with bland adroitness got Colonel Osbert outside the door.

"He's not such a fool as he looks," Reggie murmured. "But there's better brains in it than his, Lomas old thing. A bad business, quite a bad business."

And then a clerk came in. Lomas read the letter he brought and said: "Good Gad! You're an offensive person, Fortune. Why did you tell me to go to the Foreign Office? Here is the Foreign Office. Now we shall be in the affair for life. The Foreign Office wants me to see His Excellency Mustapha Firouz."

"Accompanied by Sindbad the Sailor and Chu Chin Chow?" said Reggie. "Who is he?"

"Oh, he's quite real. He's the Median Minister. He—Why what is it now?" The question was to the clerk, who had come back with a card.

"Says he's anxious to see you immediately, sir. It's very urgent, and he won't keep you long."

"Major Dean," Lomas read, and lifted an eyebrow.

"Oh rather. Let 'em all come," said Reggie.

It was Major Dean, and Major Dean ill at ease. He had a difficulty in beginning. He discovered Reggie. "Hallo! I say, can you tell me anything?" he blurted out.

"I can't," said Reggie sharply. "I don't know why your father died," and Major Dean winced.

"I thought you had something to tell us, Major," Lomas said.

"Do you believe he was murdered? I've a right to ask that."

"But it's a very grave suggestion," Lomas purred. "Do you know of anyone who had a motive for killing your father?"

"It's this filthy mystery," the Major cried. "If he was murdered, I suppose he was poisoned. But how?"

"Or why?" said Reggie.

The Major fidgeted. "I dare say he knew too much," he said. "You know he was the adviser to the Median Government. He had some pretty serious stuff through his hands. I don't know what. He was always great on official secrecy. But I know he thought it was pretty damning for some one."

"Ah, thanks very much," Lomas said.

But the Major seemed unable to go.

"I mean to say, make sure you have all his papers and stick to 'em."

Lomas and Reggie studied him. "I wonder why you say that?" Lomas asked. "The papers would naturally pass to Colonel Osbert."

"I know. Osbert was the guv'nor's best pal, worse luck. I wouldn't trust him round the corner. That's what I mean. Now I've done it, I suppose"; he gave a grim chuckle. "It is done, anyway"; and he was in a hurry to go.

Reggie stood up and stretched himself. "This is pretty thick," said he, "and we've got His Excellency the Pasha of Nine Tales on the doorstep."

Into the room was brought a man who made them feel short, a towering man draped in folds of white. Above that flowing raiment rose a majestic head, a head finely proportioned, framed in hair and beard of black strewn with grey. The face was aquiline and bold, but of a singular calm, and the dark eyes were veiled in thought. He bowed to each man twice, sat down and composed his robe about him, and it was long before he spoke. "I thank you for your great courtesy": each word came alone as if it was hard to him. "I have this to say. He who is gone he was the friend of my people. To him we turned always and he did not fail. In him we had our trust. Now, sir, I must tell you we have our enemies, who are also, as it seems to us, your enemies. Those whom you call the Turks, they would do evil to us which would be evil to you. Of this we had writings in their hands and the hands of those they use. These I gave to him who is gone that he should tell us what we should do. For your ways are not our ways nor your law our law. Now he is gone, and I am troubled lest those papers fall again into the hands of the Turks."

"Who is it that Your Excellency fears? Can you tell me of any man?" Lomas said.

"I know of none here. For the Turks are not here in the open and this is a great land of many people. Yet in all lands all things can be bought at a price. Even life and death. This only I say. If our papers go to your King and the Ministers of your King it is well and very well. If they are rendered to me that also may be well. But if they go I know not where, I say this is not just."

"I can promise Your Excellency they will go before the Foreign Office."

The Median stood up and bowed. "In England I never seek justice in vain," he said.

And when he was gone, "Good Gad, how little he knows," said Lomas. "Well, Fortune?" but Reggie only lit a cigar and curled himself up on the sofa. "What I like about you is that you never say I told you so. But you did. It is a Foreign Office touch," and still Reggie silently smoked. "Why, the thing's clear enough, isn't it?"

"Clear?" said Reggie. "Oh Peter! Clear?"

"Well, Sir Arthur had in his hands papers damaging to these blood-and-thunder Young Turks. It occurred to them that if he could die suddenly they might arrange to get the papers into their hands. So Sir Arthur is murdered, and either Osbert the executor or Major Dean the son is bribed to hand over the papers."

"In the words of the late Tennyson," said Reggie,

"And if it is so, so it is, you know;
And if it be so, so be it.

But it's not interesting, Lomas old thing."

"It would be interesting to hear you find a flaw in it," said Lomas.

Reggie shook his head. "Nary flaw."

"For my part," said Lomas with some heat, "I prefer to understand why a crime was committed. I find it useful. But I am only a policeman."

"And so say all of us." Reggie sat up. "Then why talk like a politician? Who did it and how are we going to do him in? That's our little job."

"Whoever it was, we've bilked him," said Lomas. "He has got nothing for his pains. The papers will go before the Foreign Office and then back to the Median Legation. A futile crime. I find a good deal of satisfaction in that."

"You're easy pleased then." Reggie's amiability was passing away. "A futile crime: thanks to the active and intelligent police force. But damn it, the man was murdered."

"My dear Fortune, can I help it? It's not the first and it won't be the last murder in which there is no evidence. You're pleased to be bitter about it. But you can't even tell me how the man was murdered. A poison unknown to the twentieth-century expert. No doubt that annoys you. But you needn't turn and rend me. There is also one more murderer unknown to the twentieth-century policeman. But I can't make evidence any more than you. We suspect either Osbert or Major Dean had a hand in it. But we don't know which and we don't know that either was the murderer. If we could prove that they were mixed up with the Young Turks, if we knew the man they dealt with we should have no case against them. Why, if we could find some Young Turk hireling was in the Royal Enclosure we should have no proof he was the murderer. We couldn't have," Lomas shrugged. "Humanly speaking, it's a case in which there can be no conviction."

"My only aunt, don't I know that?" Reggie cried. "And do you remember what the old Caliph said, 'In England I never seek justice in vain'? Well, that stings, Lomas-humanly speaking."

"Great heavens, what am I to do? What do you want to do?"

Reggie Fortune looked at him. The benign face of Reggie Fortune was set in hard lines. "There's something about the voice of a brother's blood crying from the ground," he said slowly.

"My dear fellow! Oh, my dear fellow, if you are going to preach," Lomas protested.

"I'm not. I'm going to tea," said Reggie Fortune. "Elise has got the trick of some new cakes. They're somewhat genial."

They did not meet again till the inquest.

It was horribly hot in court. The newspaper reporters of themselves would have filled, if given adequate space, a larger room. They sat in each other's pockets and thus yielded places to the general public, represented by a motley collection of those whom the coroner's officer permitted himself to call Nosey Parkers: frocks which might have come out of a revue chorus beside frocks which would well become a charwoman. And the Hon. Sidney Lomas murmured in the ear of his henchman Superintendent Bell, "I see several people who ought to be hanged, Bell, but no one who will give us the chance."

Mr. Reginald Fortune, that eminent surgeon, pathologist and what not, called to the witness-box, was languid and visibly bored with the whole affair. He surveyed the court in one weary, dreamy glance and gazed at the coroner as if seeking, but without hope, some reason for his unpleasant existence. Yes, he had seen Sir Arthur immediately after death. He had formed the opinion that Sir Arthur died of asphyxia and heart failure. Yes, heart failure and asphyxia. He was, however, surprised.

From the reporters' table there was a general look of hungry interest. But one young gentleman who had grown fat in the service of crime breathed heavily in his neighbour's ear: "Nothing doing: I know old Fortune. This is a wash-out."

Mr. Fortune had lost interest in his own evidence. He was looking sleepily round the court. The coroner had to recall his wandering mind. "You were surprised, Mr. Fortune?"

"Oh, ah. Well, I couldn't explain the suddenness of the attack, the symptoms and so forth. So with the assistance of Dr. Harvey I made a further examination. We went into the matter with care and used every known test. There is no evidence to be found that any other factor was present than the natural causes of death."

"But that does not explain the sudden failure of the heart."

"I don't explain it," said Reggie. "I can't."

"Medicine," said the coroner sagely, "still has its mysteries. We must remember, gentlemen, that Sir Arthur had already completed our allotted span, the Psalmist's threescore years and ten. I am much obliged to you, Mr. Fortune."

And after that, as the fat young gentleman complained, there was nothing in it. The jury found that Sir Arthur's death was from natural causes and that they sympathized with the family. So much for the Ascot mystery. There remains the sequel.

When the court broke up and sought, panting, the open air, "He is neat, sir, isn't he?" said Lomas's henchman, Superintendent Bell. "Very adroit, is Mr. Fortune. That couldn't have been much better done." And Lomas smiled. It was in each man's simple heart that the Criminal Investigation Department was well rid of a bad business. They sought Reggie to give him lunch.

But Reggie was already outside; Reggie was strolling, as one for whom time has no meaning, towards the station. He was caught up by the plump young reporter, who would like you to call him a crime specialist. "Well, Mr. Fortune," he said in his ingratiating way, "good morning. How are you, sir? I say, you have put it across us in the Dean case."

The crime specialist then had opportunities for psychological study as Mr. Fortune's expression performed a series of quick changes. But it settled down into bland and amiable surprise. "My dear fellow," said Mr. Fortune, "how are you? But what's the trouble? There's nothing in the Dean case, never was."

"No, that's just it. And we were all out for a first-class crime story. After all the talk there's been, natural causes is pretty paltry."

Reggie laughed. "Sorry, sorry. We can't make crimes for you. But why did you talk? There was nothing to talk about."

"I say, you know, that's a bit thick," the crime specialist protested.

"My dear chap," said Reggie modestly, "if the doctor on the spot hadn't happened to be me, you would never have thought of the case. Nothing else in it."

"Oh, well, come now, Mr. Fortune! I mean to say-what about the C.I.D. holding up all the old man's papers and turning down his executor?"

Reggie was not surprised, he was bewildered. "Say it again slowly and distinctly," he entreated, and when that was done he was as one who tries not to laugh. "And very nice too. My dear fellow, what more do you want? There's a story for you."

"Well, it's never been officially denied," said the young man.

"Fancy that!" Reggie chuckled.

"But between ourselves, Mr. Fortune ——"

"It's a great story," Reggie chuckled. "But really-Well, I ask you!" and he slid away.

In the hotel lounge he found Bell and Lomas and cocktails. "Pleasure before business, as ever," he reproached them, and ordered one for himself.

"And what have you been doing, then?" Lomas asked.

"I have been consoling the Fourth Estate. That great institution the Press, Mr. Lomas, sir. Through one of Gilligan's young lions. Out of the mouths of babes and sucklings ——"

"I wish you wouldn't talk to reporters," Lomas complained.

"You're so haughty. By the way, what was Ludlow Blenkinhorn doing here?" He referred to a solicitor of more ability than standing. "Osbert was here and his solicitor, the young Deans and their solicitor. Who was old Blenkinhorn representing?"

Bell and Lomas looked at each other. "Didn't see the fellow," said Lomas.

"Mr. Fortune's quite right, sir. Blenkinhorn was standing with the public. And that's odd, too."

"Highly odd. Lomas, my dear old thing, I wish you'd watch Blenkinhorn's office and Osbert's flat for any chaps who look a bit exotic, a bit foreign-and follow him up if you find one."

Lomas groaned. "Surely we've done with the case."

"Ye-es. But there's some fellow who hasn't. And he has a pretty taste in poisons. And he's still wanting papers."

"We've nothing to act on, you know," Lomas protested.

"Oh, not a thing, not a thing. But he might have." Lomas nodded and Superintendent Bell went to the telephone.

When Mr. Fortune read "The Daily Post" in the morning he smiled upon his devilled kidneys. Its report of the inquest was begun with a little pompous descriptive work. "The mystery of the Ascot Tragedy was solved yesterday. In the cold sanity of the coroner's court the excitement of the last few days received its quietus. Two minutes of scientific evidence from Mr. Fortune —" and so on until young omniscience worked up to its private little scoop. "The melodramatic rumours of sensational developments in the case have thus only availed to expose the fatuity of their inventors." (This was meant for some rival papers.) "It may now be stated bluntly that nothing in the case ever gave rise to speculation among well-informed people, and that the stories of impounding documents and so forth have no foundation in fact."

But about lunch time Mr. Fortune received a curt summons from the Hon. Sidney Lomas and instantly obeyed it. "Well, you know, I thought I should be hearing from you," he smiled. "I felt, as it were, you couldn't live without me long."

"Did you, by Jove!" said Lomas bitterly. "I've been wishing all the morning you had been dead some time. Look at that!" He tossed across the table a marked copy of "The Daily Post."

"Yes, I was enjoying that at breakfast. A noble institution, the British Press, Lomas. A great power. If you know how to use it."

"I wish to God you wouldn't spoof reporters. It's a low taste. And it's a damned nuisance. I can't contradict the rag and — —"

"No, you can't contradict it. I banked on that," Reggie chuckled.

"Did you indeed? And pray what the devil are you at? I have had Osbert here raving mad — —"

"Yes, I thought it would stir up Osbert. What's his line?"

"Wants the papers, of course. And as you very well know, confound you, they're all at the Foreign Office, the cream of them, and likely to be. He says we've no right to keep them after this. Nonsense, of course, but devilish inconvenient to answer. And at last the old man was quite pathetic, says it isn't fair to him to give out we haven't touched the papers. No more it is. He was begging me to contradict it officially. I could hardly get rid of him."

"Busy times for Lomas."

"Damme, I have been at it all the morning. Old Ludlow Blenkinhorn turned up, too."

"I have clicked, haven't I?" Reggie chuckled.

"Confound you. He says he has a client with claims on the estate and is informed by the executor that all papers have been taken by us. Now he has read your damned article and he wants to know if the executor is lying."

"That is a conundrum, isn't it? And who is Mr. Ludlow Blenkinhorn's client?"

"He didn't say, of course."

"What a surprise. And your fellows watching his office, do they say?"

Lomas took up a scrap of paper. "They have sent us something. A man of foreign or mulatto appearance called on him first thing this morning. Was followed to a Bayswater lodging-house. Is known there as Sherif. Mr. A. Sherif. Thought to be an Egyptian."

"The negro or Hamitic heel!" Reggie murmured. "Do you remember, Lomas old thing?"

"Good Gad!" Lomas dropped his eyeglass. "But what the devil can we do?"

"Watch and pray," said Reggie. "Your fellows watch Sherif and Blenkinhorn and Osbert and you pray. Do you pray much, Lomas?"

They went in fact to lunch. They were not long back when a detective speaking over the telephone reported that a man of mulatto appearance had called on Colonel Osbert. Reggie sprang up. "Come on, Lomas. We'll have them in the act and bluff the whole thing out of them."

"What act?"

"Collusion. This Egyptian-Syrian-negroid-Young Turk and the respectable executor. Come on, man."

In five minutes they were mounting to Colonel Osbert's flat. His servant could not say whether Colonel Osbert was at home. Lomas produced his card. "Colonel Osbert will see me," he announced, and fixed the man with a glassy stare.

"Well, sir, I beg pardon, sir. There's a gentleman with him."

"At once," said Lomas and walked into the hall.

The man still hesitated. From one of the rooms could be heard voices in some excitement. Lomas and Reggie made for that door. But as they approached there was a cry, a horrible shrill cry, and the sound of a scuffle. Reggie sprang forward. Some one rushed out of the room and Reggie, the smaller man, went down before him. Lomas clutched at him and was kicked in the stomach. The fellow was off. Reggie picked himself out of the hatstand and ran after him. Lomas, in a heap, gasping and hiccoughing, fumbled in his pocket. "B-b-blow," he stammered to the stupefied servant, and held out a whistle. "Like hell. Blow!"

A long peal sounded through the block of flats.

Down below a solid man strolled out of the porter's lodge just as a gentleman of dark complexion and large feet was hurrying through the door. The solid man put out a leg. Another solid man outside received the gentleman on his bosom. They had then some strenuous moments. By the time Reggie reached them three hats were on the ground, but a pair of handcuffs clasped the coffee-coloured wrists.

"His pockets," Reggie panted, "his waistcoat pockets."

The captive said something which no one understood, and struggled. One of the detectives held out a small white-metal case. Reggie took from it a hypodermic syringe. "I didn't think you were so up-to-date," said Reggie. "What did you put in it? Well, well, I suppose you won't tell me. Take him away."

He went back to find Lomas and the servant looking at Colonel Osbert. Colonel Osbert lay on the floor. There was froth at his lips and on his wrist a spot of blood. Reggie knelt down beside him....

"Too late?" Lomas said hoarsely.

Reggie rose. "Well, you can put it that way," he said. "It's the end."

In Lomas's room Reggie spread himself on a sofa and watched Lomas drink whisky and soda. "A ghastly business," Lomas said: he was still pale and unsteady. "That creature is a wild beast."

"He'll go where he belongs," said Reggie, who was eating bread and butter. "All according to plan."

"Plan? My God, the man runs amuck!"

"Oh, no, no, no. He wanted those papers for his employers. He contracted with Osbert to hand them over when Dean was dead. He murdered Dean and Osbert couldn't deliver the goods. So I told him through the papers that Osbert had them. He thought Osbert was bilking him and went to have it out with him. Osbert didn't satisfy him, he was sure he had been done and he made Osbert pay for it. All according to plan."

Lomas set down his glass. "Fortune," he said nervously, "Fortune-do you mean-when you put that in the paper-you meant the thing to end like this?"

"Well, what are we here for?" said Reggie. "But you know you're forgetting the real interest of the case."

"Am I?" said Lomas weakly.

"Yes. What is his poison?"

"Oh, good Gad," said Lomas.

CASE II

THE PRESIDENT OF SAN JACINTO

MR. REGINALD FORTUNE lay in a long chair. On his right hand a precipice fell to still black water. On his left the mountains rose into a tiara of snow. Far away in front sunlight found the green flood of a glacier. But Mr. Fortune saw none of these things. He was eating strawberries and cream.

The Hon. Sidney Lomas, Chief of the Criminal Investigation Department, disguised as a bloodthirsty fisherman, arrived stiffly but happy, and behind him a large Norwegian bore the corpses of two salmon into the farm-house. "The lord high detective," Reggie murmured. "An allegorical picture, by the late Mr. Watts."

"Great days," Lomas said, and let himself down gingerly into a chair. "Hallo, has there been a post?" He reached for one of the papers at Reggie's feet. "My country, what of thee?"

"They're at it again, Lomas. They've murdered a real live lord."

"Thank heaven I'm not there. Who is it?"

"One Carwell. In the wilds of the Midlands."

"Young Carwell? He's a blameless youth to slay. What happened?"

"They found him in his library with his head smashed. Queer case."

Lomas read the report, which had nothing more to tell. "Burglary, I suppose," he pronounced.

"Well, I have an alibi," said Reggie.

Neither the Chief of the Criminal Investigation Department nor his scientific adviser saw any reason to end a good holiday for the sake of avenging Lord Carwell. The policemen who dealt with the affair did not call for help. Mr. Fortune and Mr. Lomas continued to catch the salmon and eat the strawberries of Norway and let the world go by and became happily out of date. It was not till they were on the North Sea that they met the Carwell case again.

The Newcastle packet was rolling in a slow, heavy rhythm. Most of the passengers had succumbed. Lomas and Reggie fitted themselves and two chairs into a corner of the upper deck with all the London newspapers that were waiting for them at Bergen. Lomas, a methodical man, began at the beginning. Reggie worked back from the end. And in a moment, "My only aunt!" he said softly. "Lomas, old thing, they're doing themselves proud. Who do you think they've taken for that Carwell murder? The cousin, the heir, one Mark Carwell. This is highly intriguing."

"Good Gad!"

"As you say," Reggie agreed. "Yes. Public Prosecutor on it. Old Brunker leading for the Crown. Riding pretty hard, too. The man Mark is for it, I fear, Lomas. They do these things quite neatly without us. It's all very disheartening."

"Mark Carwell? A harum-scarum young ruffian he always was."

"Yes. Have you noticed these little things mean much? I haven't."

"What's the case?"

"The second housemaid found Lord Carwell sitting in the library with his head smashed. He was dead. The doctor came up in half an hour, found him cold, and swears he had been dead five or six hours. Cause of death-brain injury from the blow given by some heavy, blunt instrument. No one in the house had heard a sound. No sign of burglary, no weapon. There was a small house-party, the man Mark, the girl Carwell was engaged to, Lady Violet Barclay and her papa and mamma, and Sir Brian Carwell-that's the contractor, some sort of distant cousin. Mark was left with Lord Carwell when the rest of them went to bed. Lady Violet and papa and mamma say they heard a noisy quarrel. Violet says Carwell had told her before that Mark was writing to him for money to get married on, and Carwell didn't approve of the girl."

"I don't fancy Carwell would approve of the kind of girl Mark would want to marry."

"Yes, that's what the fair Violet implies. She seems to be a good hater. She did her little best to hang Mark."

"Why, if he killed her man, can you wonder?"

"Oh, I don't wonder. But I wouldn't like to get in her way myself. Not really a nice girl. She swore Mark had been threatening Carwell, and Carwell was afraid of him. The prosecution put in a letter of Mark's which talked wild about doing something vague and desperate if Carwell didn't stump up."

"Did Mark go into the box?"

"Yes. That was his error. I'm afraid he isn't respectable, Lomas. He showed no seemly grief. He made it quite clear that he had no use for Hugo, Lord Carwell. He rather suggested that Hugo had lived to spite him, and got killed to spite him. He admitted all Lady Violet's evidence and underlined it. He said Hugo had been more against him than ever since she came into the family. He owned to the quarrel of Hugo's last night. Only he swore that he left the man alive."

"Well, he did his best to hang himself."

"As you say. A bold, bad fellow. That's all, except that cousin Mark had a big stick, a loaded stick with a knob head, and he took it down to Carwell Hall."

"What's the verdict?"

"To be continued in our next. The judge was going to sum up in the morning. In the paper we haven't got."

Lomas lay back and watched the grey sea rise into sight as the boat rolled to starboard. "What do you make of it, Fortune?"

"There's the rudiments of a case," said Reggie. "The Carwell estate is entailed. Mark is the heir. He didn't love the man. The man was going to marry and that would wash out Mark. Mark was the last man with him, unless there is some hard lying. They had a row about money and girls, which are always infuriating, and Mark had a weapon handy which might have killed him. And nobody else had any motive, there's no evidence of anybody else in the business. Yes, the rudiments of a case."

"I don't see the rudiments of a defence."

"The defence is that Mark says that he didn't."

"Quite, quite," Lomas nodded. "It's not the strongest case in the world, but I have had convictions on worse. The jury will go by what they made of Mark in the box."

"And hang him for his face." Reggie turned over a paper and held out the portrait of a bull-necked, square-headed young man.

"I wouldn't say they'd be wrong," Lomas said. "Who's the judge? Maine? He'll keep 'em straight."

"I wonder. What is straight, Lomas?"

"My dear fellow, it all turns on the way this lad gave his evidence, and that you can't tell from a report."

"He don't conciliate me," Reggie murmured. "Yet I like evidence, Lomas."

"Why, this is adequate, if it's true. And Mark didn't challenge it."

"I know. Adequate is the word. Just enough and nothing more. That's unusual, Lomas. Well, well. What about tea?"

They picked their way over some prostrate bodies to the saloon and again gave up the Carwell case.

But when the boat had made her slow way through the clatter of the Tyne, Reggie was quick to intercept the first customs officer on board. "I say, what was the result of that murder trial?"

The man laughed. "Thought you wanted the 3.30 winner, you were so keen, sir. Oh, Mark Carwell's guilty, of course. His mother's white-haired boy, he is. Not 'alf."

"The voice of the people," said Lomas, in Reggie's ear.

On the way to London they read the judge's summing up, an oration lucid and fair but relentless.

"He had no doubt," Reggie said.

"And a good judge too," Lomas tossed the paper aside. "Thank heaven they got it out of the way without bothering me."

"You are an almost perfect official," said Reggie with reverence.

In the morning when Reggie came down to his breakfast in London he was told that some one had rung up to know if he was back in England yet. He was only half-way through his omelet when the name of Miss Joan Amber was brought to him.

Every one who likes to see a beautiful actress act, and many who don't care whether she can act or not, know what Miss Amber looks like, that large young woman with the golden eyes whom Reggie hurried to welcome. He held her hand rather a long while. "The world is very good to-day," he said, and inspected her. "You don't need a holiday, Miss Amber."

"You've had too much, Mr. Fortune."

"Have you been kind enough to want me?"

"I really meant that you looked — —" she made a large gesture.

"No, no-not fat," Reggie protested. "Only genial. I expand in your presence."

"Well-round," said Miss Amber. "And my presence must be very bad for you."

"No, not bad for me-only crushing."

"Well, I did sometimes notice you were away. And I want you now. For a friend of mine. Will you help her?"

"When did I ever say No to you?"

"Bless you," said Miss Amber. "It's the Carwell case."

"Oh, my prophetic soul," Reggie groaned. "But what in wonder have you to do with the Carwell case?"

"I know Nan Nest. She's the girl Mark Carwell is going to marry."

"Do you mind if you sit down?" said Reggie, and wandered away to the window. "You're disturbing to the intellect, Miss Amber. Let us be calm. You shouldn't talk about people marrying people and look like that." Miss Amber smiled at his back. She has confessed to moments in which she would like to be Reggie Fortune's mother. "Yes. Well now, does Miss Amber happen to know the man Mark?"

"I've met him. He's not a bad fellow. A first-class fighting-subaltern. That sort of thing."

Reggie nodded. "That's his public form too."

"Oh, Mr. Fortune, he's absolutely straight. Not a very wise youth, of course. You know, I could imagine him killing his cousin, but what I can't imagine is that he would ever say he didn't if he did."

"Yes. There weren't any women on the jury?"

"Don't sneer."

"I never do when you're listening. That was a scientific statement. Now, what's Miss Nest like?"

"Like a jolly schoolboy. Or she was, poor child. Oh, they would have been splendidly happy, if that tiresome man had set Mark up somewhere in the country instead of getting himself murdered."

Reggie smiled sadly. "Don't say that to anyone but me. Or let her say it. Why did the tiresome man object to her? I suppose it's true that he did?"

"Oh heavens, yes. Because she's on the stage. She plays little parts, you know, flappers and such. She's quite good as herself. She can't act."

"What was the late Carwell? What sort of fellow? That didn't come out at the trial."

"A priceless prig, Mark says. I suppose he was the last survivor of our ancient aristocracy. Poor Mark!"

"I wonder," Reggie murmured.

"What?"

"Well" —he spread out his hands —"everything. You haven't exactly cleared it up, have you?"

"Mark told Nan he didn't do it," she said quietly, and Reggie looked into her eyes. "Oh, can't you see? That's to trust to. That's sure." Reggie turned away. "You will help her?" the low voice came again.

And at last, "My dear, I daren't say so," Reggie said. "You mustn't tell her to hope anything. I'll go over all the case. But the man is condemned."

"Why, but there's a court of appeal."

"Only for something new. And I don't see it."

"Mark didn't kill him!" she cried.

Reggie spread out his hands. "That's faith."

"Mr. Fortune! When I said I had come about the Carwell case, you said, 'Oh, my prophetic soul!' You don't believe the evidence, then. You never did. You always thought there was something they didn't find out."

"I don't know. I don't know," Reggie said slowly. "That's the last word now. And it may be the last word in the end."

"You!" she said, and held out her hand.

When she was gone, Reggie stood looking at the place where she had sat. "God help us," he said, rare words on his lips. And the place he went to was Scotland Yard.

Lomas was occupied with other sublime officials. So Superintendent Bell reported. He had also been telephoning for Mr. Fortune. Mr. Fortune was admitted and found himself before a large red truculent man who glared. "Hallo, Finch. Is this a council of war?" said Mr. Fortune; for at that date Mr. Montague Finchampstead was the Public Prosecutor.

"Lomas tells me"—Finchampstead has a bullying manner—"you've formed an opinion on the evidence in the Carwell case."

"Then he knows more than I do. The evidence was all right-what there was of it."

"The chain is complete," Finchampstead announced.

"Yes. Yes. If you don't pull it hard."

"Well, no one did pull it."

"That's what I'm pointing out, Finch," said Reggie sweetly. "Why are you so cross?"

"The trouble is, Fortune, the Carwell butler's bolted," Lomas said.

Reggie walked across the room and took one of Lomas's cigars and lit it, and made himself comfortable in his chair. "That's a new fact," he said softly.

"Nonsense," Finchampstead cried. "It's irrelevant. It doesn't affect the issue. The verdict stands."

"I noticed you didn't call the butler at the trial," Reggie murmured.

"Why the devil should we? He knew nothing."

"Yet he bolts."

Lomas smiled. "The unfortunate thing is, Fortune, he bolted before the trial was over. At the end of the second day the local police were told that he had vanished. The news was passed on to Finchampstead. But the defence was not informed. And it didn't come out at the trial."

"Well, well. I thought you were riding rather hard, Finch. You were."

"Rubbish. The case was perfectly clear. The disappearance of the butler doesn't affect it-if he has disappeared. The fellow may very well have gone off on some affair of his own, and turn up again in a day or two. And if he doesn't, it's nothing to the purpose. The butler was known to have a kindness for Mark Carwell. If we never hear of him again I shall conclude that he had a hand in the murder, and when he saw the case was going against Mark thought he had better vanish."

"Theory number two," Reggie murmured.

"What do you mean?"

"Your first was that the butler knew nothing. Your second is that he knows too much. Better choose which leg you'll stand on in the Court of Appeal."

Finchampstead glared.

"In the meantime, Finch, we'll try to find the butler for you," said Lomas cheerfully.

"And I think I'll have a look at the evidence," Reggie murmured.

"There is no flaw in the evidence," Finchampstead boomed.

"Well, not till you look at it."

Finchampstead with some explosions of disgust removed himself.

"Zeal, all zeal," said Reggie sadly. "Well-meaning man. Only one idea at a time. And sometimes a wrong un."

"He's a lawyer by nature," Lomas apologized. "You always rub him up the wrong way. He don't like the scientific mind. What?" Bell had come in to give him a visiting card. He read out, "Sir Brian Carwell." He looked at Reggie. "Now which side is he on?"

"One moment. Who exactly is he? Some sort of remote cousin?"

"Yes. He comes of a younger branch. People say the brains of the Carwell's went to them. His father was the engineer, old Ralph Carwell. This man's an engineering contractor. He made his pile over South American railways."

"You wouldn't say he was passionately interested in the late Lord Carwell or Cousin Mark."

There came in a lean man with an air of decision and authority, but older than his resilient vigour suggested, for his hair was much sprinkled with grey, and in his brown face, about the eyes and mouth, the wrinkles were many. He was exact with the formalities of introduction and greeting, but much at his ease, and then, "I had better explain who I am, Mr. Lomas."

"Oh, we've heard of Sir Brian Carwell."

"Thanks. But I dare say you don't know my private affairs. I'm some sort of fifteenth cousin of these two unfortunate young fellows. And just now I happen to be the acting head of the family. I'm not the next heir, of course. That's old Canon Carwell. But I was on the spot when this thing happened. After his arrest Mark asked me to take charge for him, and the Canon wished me to act. That's my position. Well, I carried on to keep things as they were at the Hall and on the estate. Several of the servants want to quit, of course, but they haven't gone yet. The butler was a special case. He told me he had given Hugo notice some time before. I could find no record, but it was possible enough, and as he only wanted to retire and settle down in the neighbourhood, I made no difficulty. So he set himself up in lodgings in the village. He was looking about for a house, he told me. I suppose he had done pretty well. He had been in service at the Hall thirty or forty years, poor devil. What a life! He knew Hugo and Mark much better than I do, had known 'em all their young lives. He knew all the family affairs inside and out. One night the people where he was lodging went round to the police to say he'd gone out and not come back. He hasn't come back yet."

"And what do you conclude, Sir Brian?"

"I'll be damned if I know what I conclude. That's your business, isn't it?"

"Not without some facts," said Lomas. "When did he leave the Hall?"

"After Mark was arrested. May 13. And he disappeared on the evening of the second day of the trial."

"That would be when it looked certain that Mark would be found guilty. Why did he wait till then?"

Sir Brian laughed. "If I knew that, I suppose I shouldn't be here. I'm asking you to find him."

"Quite, quite," Lomas agreed. "The local police knew of his disappearance at once?"

"I said so. I wish I had known as soon. The police didn't bother to mention it at the trial. It might have made some difference to the verdict, Mr. Lomas."

"That's matter of opinion, of course," said Lomas. "I wasn't in England myself. I needn't tell you that it's open to the defence to appeal against the conviction."

"Is it?" Sir Brian's shadowed eyes grew smaller. "You don't know Mark, Mr. Lomas. If I were to tell you Mark refuses to make an appeal on this ground because it would be putting the murder on the butler, what would you say?"

"Good Gad!" was what Lomas did say. He lay back and put up his eyeglass and looked from Sir Brian to Reggie and back again. "You mean Mark admits he is guilty?"

"Guilty be damned," said Sir Brian. "No, sir, I mean Mark liked the wretched fellow and won't hear of anything against him. Mark's a fool. But that's not a reason for hanging him. I say you got your conviction by suppressing evidence. It's up to you to review the case."

"Still, Lord Carwell was killed," said Lomas gently, "and somebody killed him. Who was it?"

"Not Mark. He hasn't got it in him, I suppose he never hit a fellow who couldn't hit back in his life."

"But surely," Lomas purred, "if there was a quarrel, Lord Carwell might——"

"Hugo was a weed," Sir Brian pronounced. "Mark never touched him, my friend."

"Yes, yes, very natural you should think so," Lomas shifted his papers. "Of course you won't expect me to say anything, Sir Brian. And what exactly is it you want me to do?"

Sir Brian laughed. "My dear sir, it's not for me to tell you your duty. I put it to you that a man has disappeared, and that his disappearance makes hay of the case on which the Crown convicted a cousin of mine of murder. What you do about it is your affair."

"You may rely upon it, Sir Brian," said Lomas in his most official manner, "the affair will be thoroughly investigated."

"I expected no less, Mr. Lomas." And Sir Brian ceremoniously but briskly took his leave.

After which, "Good Gad!" said Lomas again, and stared at Reggie Fortune.

"Nice restful companion, isn't he? Yes. The sort of fellow that has made Old England great."

"Oh, I don't mind him. He could be dealt with. But he's right, confound him. The case is a most unholy mess."

"Well, well," said Reggie placidly. "You must rub it out, dear, and do it again."

"If everybody had tried to muddle it they couldn't have done worse."

Reggie stared at him. "Yes. Yes, you have your moments, Lomas," he said.

"Suppose the butler did the murder. Why in the world should he wait to run away till Mark was certain to be found guilty?"

"And suppose he didn't, why did he run away at all? You can make up quite a lot of riddles in this business. Why should anyone but Mark do it? Why is Mark so mighty tender of the butler's reputation? Why is anything?"

"Yes, it's all crazy-except Sir Brian. He's reasonable enough, confound him."

"Yes. Yes, these rational men are a nuisance to the police. Well, well, begin again at the beginning."

"I wish I knew where it did begin."

"My dear fellow! Are we down-hearted? I'll have a look at the medical evidence. You go over Carwell Hall and the butler's digs with a small tooth comb."

But the first thing which Mr. Fortune did was to send a note to Miss Amber.

My dear Child —

Mark can appeal. The ground for it is the disappearance of the Carwell butler-and a good ground.

But he must appeal. Tell Miss Nest.

R. F.

Two days afterwards he went again to Scotland Yard summoned to a conference of the powers. The public prosecutor's large and florid face had no welcome for him. "Any more new facts, Finch?" he said cheerfully.

"Mark Carwell has entered an appeal," Mr. Finchampstead boomed. "On the ground of the butler's disappearance."

"Fancy that!" Reggie murmured, and lit a cigar. "Sir Brian doesn't seem to have been very well informed, Lomas."

"The boy's come to his senses, I suppose. But we haven't found the butler. He left no papers behind him. All he did leave was his clothes and about a hundred pounds in small notes."

"So he didn't take his ready money. That's interesting."

"Well, not all of it. He left another hundred or so in the savings bank, and some small investments in building societies and so forth —a matter of five hundred. Either he didn't mean to vanish, or he was in the deuce of a hurry to go."

"Yes. Yes, there's another little point. Five or six hundred isn't much to retire on. Why was he in such a hurry to retire?"

"He may have had more than we can trace, of course. He may have gone off with some Carwell property. But there is no evidence of anything being stolen."

"The plain fact is," Finchampstead boomed, "you have found out nothing but that he's gone. We knew that before."

"And it's a pity you kept it dark," said Lomas acidly. "You wouldn't have had an appeal to fight."

"The case against Mark Carwell is intrinsically as strong as ever," Finchampstead pronounced. "There is no reason whatever to suspect the butler, he had no motive for murder, he gained nothing by it, his disappearance is most naturally accounted for by an accident."

"Yes, you'll have to say all that in the Court of Appeal. I don't think it will cut much ice."

"I am free to admit that his disappearance is an awkward complication in the case," Finchampstead's oratory rolled on. "But surely, Lomas, you have formed some theory in explanation?"

Lomas shook his head.

"We've had too much theory, Finch," said Reggie cheerfully. "Let's try some facts. I want the body exhumed."

The eyes of Mr. Finchampstead goggled. His large jaw fell.

"Good Gad, you don't doubt he's dead?" Lomas cried.

"Oh, he'll be dead all right. I want to know how he died."

"Are you serious?" Finchampstead mourned. "Really, Fortune, this is not a matter for frivolity. The poor fellow was found dead with one side of his head beaten in. There can be no dispute how he died. I presume you have taken the trouble to read the medical evidence."

"I have. That's what worries me. I've seen the doctors you called. Dear old things."

"Very sound men. And of the highest standing," Finchampstead rebuked him.

"As you say. They know a fractured skull when they see it. They would see everything they looked for. But they didn't look for what they didn't see."

"May I ask what you mean?"

"Any other cause of death."

"The cause was perfectly plain. There was nothing else to look for."

"Yes. Yes," Reggie lay back and blew smoke. "That's the sort of reasoning that got you this verdict. Look here, Finch. That smashed head would have killed him all right, but it shouldn't have killed him so quick. He ought to have lingered unconscious a long while. And he had been dead hours when they found him. We have to begin again from the beginning. I want an order for exhumation."

"Better ask for a subpoena for his soul."

"That's rather good, Finch," Reggie smiled. "You're beginning to take an interest in the case."

"If you could take the evidence of the murdered," said Lomas, "a good many convictions for murder would look rather queer."

Mr. Finchampstead was horrified. "I conceive," he announced with dignity, "that a trial in an English court is a practically perfect means of discovering the truth."

Reverently then they watched him go. And when he was gone, "He's a wonderful man," said Reggie. "He really believes that."

The next morning saw Mr. Fortune, escorted by Superintendent Bell, arrive at Carwell Hall. It stands in what Mr. Fortune called a sluggish country, a country of large rolling fields and slow rivers. The air was heavy and blurred all colour and form. Mr. Fortune arrived at Carwell Hall feeling as if he had eaten too much, a sensation rare in him, which he resented. He was hardly propitiated by the house, though others have rejoiced in it. It was built under the Tudors out of the spoils and, they say, with the stones of an abbey. Though some eighteenth-century ruffian played tricks with it, its mellow walls still speak of an older, more venturous world. It is a place of studied charm, gracious and smiling, but in its elaboration of form and ornament offering a thousand things to look at, denies itself as a whole, evasive and strange.

Reggie got out of the car and stood back to survey it. "Something of everything, isn't it, Bell? Like a Shakespeare play. Just the place to have a murder in one room with a children's party in the next, and a nice girl making love on the stairs, and father going mad in the attics."

"I rather like Shakespeare myself, sir," said Superintendent Bell,

"You're so tolerant," said Reggie, and went in.

A new butler said that Sir Brian was expecting them. Sir Brian was brusquely civil. He was very glad to find that the case was being reopened. The whole place was at their orders. Anything he could do — —

"I thought I might just look round," Reggie said. "We are rather after the fair, though." He did not think it necessary to tell Sir Brian that Lord Carwell's body would be dug up that night.

They were taken across a hall with a noble roof of hammer beams to the place of the murder. The library was panelled in oak, which at a man's height from the ground flowered into carving. The ceiling was moulded into a hundred coats of arms, each blazoned with its right device, and the glow and colour of them, scarlet and bright blue and gold, filled the room. Black presses with vast locks stood here and there. A stool was on either side the great open hearth. By the massive table a stern fifteenth-century chair was set.

Bell gazed about him and breathed heavily. "Splendid room, sir," he said. "Quite palatial."

"But it's not what I'd want after dinner myself," Reggie murmured.

"I've no use for the place," said Sir Brian. "But it suited Hugo. He would never have a thing changed. He was really a survival. Poor old Hugo."

"He was sitting here?" Reggie touched the chair.

"So they tell me. I didn't see him till some time after the girl found him. You'd better hear what she has to say."

A frightened and agitated housemaid testified that his lordship had been sitting in that chair bent over the table and his head rested on it, and the left side of his head was all smashed, and on the table was a pool of his blood. She would never forget it, never. She became aware of Reggie's deepening frown. "That's the truth, sir," she cried, "so help me God, it is."

"I know, I know," said Reggie. "No blood anywhere else? No other marks in the room?"

There hadn't been anything. She had cleaned the room herself. And it had been awful. She hadn't slept a night since. And so on till she was got rid of.

"Well?" said Sir Brian. "What's the expert make of her?"

Reggie was looking at the table and fingering it. He looked up suddenly. "Oh, she's telling the truth," he said. "And that's that."

The lunch bell was ringing. Sir Brian hoped they would stay at the Hall. They did stay to lunch and talked South America, of which Sir Brian's knowledge was extensive and peculiar. After lunch they smoked on the terrace and contemplated through the haze the Carwell acres. "Yes, it's all Carwell land as far as you see-if you could see anything," Sir Brian laughed. "And nothing to see at that. Flat arable. I couldn't live in the place. I never feel awake here. But the family's been on the ground four hundred years. They didn't own the estate. The estate owned them. Well, I suppose one life's as good as another if you like it. This isn't mine. Watching Englishmen grow wheat! My God! That just suited Hugo. Poor old Hugo!"

"Had the butler anything against him, sir?" Bell ventured.

"I can't find it. The butler was just a butler. I never saw a man more so. And Hugo, well, he didn't know servants existed unless they didn't answer the bell. But he was a queer fellow. No notion of anybody having rights against him. He wouldn't let you get near him. I've seen that make quiet men mad."

"Meaning anyone in particular, sir?" Bell said.

"Oh Lord, no. Speaking generally." He looked at Bell with a shrewd smile. "Haven't you found that in your job?" And Bell laughed. "Yes, I'm afraid I don't help you much. Are you going to help Mark? Where is the butler?"

"Yes. Yes, we are rather wasting time, aren't we?" Reggie stretched himself. "It's too soothing, Sir Brian. Can we walk across the park? I hate exercise, but man must live."

"I don't think anyone would have to murder me if I stayed here long," Sir Brian started up. "I'll show you the way. We can send your car round to the village."

Over immemorial turf they went their warm way. A herd of deer looked at them critically, and concluded they were of no importance. "Pretty creatures," said Superintendent Bell.

"I'd as soon keep white mice," said Sir Brian, and discoursed of the wilder deer of other lands till he discovered that Reggie was left behind.

Reggie was wandering off towards a little building away in a hollow among trees. It was low, it was of unhewn stone bonded with lines of red tile or brick, only a little above the moss-grown roof rose a thin square tower. The tiny rounded windows showed walls of great thickness and over its one door was a mighty round arch, much wrought.

"Does the old place take your fancy?" Sir Brian said.

"How did that get here?" said Reggie.

"Well, you've got me on my blind side," Sir Brian confessed. "We call it the old church. I dare say it's as old as the Hall."

"The Hall's a baby to it," said Reggie angrily. "The porch is Norman. There's Saxon work in that tower. And that tile is Roman."

Sir Brian laughed. "What about the Greeks and the Hebrews? Give them a look in." Reggie was not pleased with him. "Sorry, afraid these things don't mean much to me. I don't know how it began."

"It may have been a shrine or a chapel over some sacred place."

"Haven't a notion. They say it used to be the village church. One of my revered ancestors stopped the right of way-didn't like the people disturbing his poultry, I suppose-and built 'em a new church outside the park."

"Priceless," Reggie murmured.

"What, the place or my ancestors?"

"Well, both, don't you think?"

For the rest of the way Sir Brian told strange stories of the past of the family of Carwell.

"He's a good talker, sir," said Superintendent Bell, when they had left him at the park gate and were in their car. "Very pleasant company. But you've something on your mind."

"The chair," Reggie mumbled. "Why was the man in his chair?"

"Lord Carwell, sir?" Bell struggled to adjust his mind. "Well, he was. That girl was telling the truth."

"I know, I know. That's the difficulty. You smash the side of a man's head in. He won't sit down to think about it."

"Perhaps he was sitting when he was hit."

"Then he'd be knocked over just the same."

"I suppose the murderer might have picked him up."

"He might. But why? Why?"

Superintendent Bell sighed heavily. "I judge we've some way to go, sir. And we don't seem to get any nearer the butler."

"Your job," said Reggie, and again the Superintendent sighed.

That night through a drizzling rain, lanterns moved in the village churchyard. The vault in which the Carwells of a hundred and fifty years lie crumbling was opened, and out of it a coffin was borne away. One man lingered in the vault holding a lantern high. He moved from one coffin to another, and came up again to the clean air and the rain. "All present and correct," he said. "No deception, Bell."

Superintendent Bell coughed. Sometimes he thinks Mr. Fortune lacking in reverence.

"Division of labour," Reggie sank into the cushions of the car and lit a pipe, "the division of labour is the great principle of civilization. Perhaps you didn't know that? In the morning I will look at the corpse and you will look for the butler."

"Well, sir, I don't care for my job, but I wouldn't have yours for a hundred pounds."

"Yet it has a certain interest," Reggie murmured, "for that poor devil with the death sentence on him."

To their hotel in Southam Reggie Fortune came back on the next day rather before lunch time.

"Finished at the mortuary, sir?" said Bell. "I thought you looked happy."

"Not happy. Only pleased with myself. A snare, Bell, a snare. Have you found the butler?"

Bell shook his head. "It's like a fairy tale, sir. He went out on that evening, walked down the village street, and that's the last of him they know. He might have gone to the station, he might have gone on the Southam motor-bus. They can't swear he didn't, but nobody saw him. They've searched the whole country-side and dragged the river. If you'll tell me what to do next, I'll be glad."

"Sir Brian's been asking for me, they say," said Reggie. "I think we'll go and call on Sir Brian."

They took sandwiches and their motor to Carwell Hall. The new butler told them Sir Brian had driven into Southam and was not yet back. "Oh, we've crossed him, I suppose," Reggie said. "We might stroll in the park till he's back. Ah, can we get into the old church?"

The butler really couldn't say, and remarked that he was new to the place.

"Oh, it's no matter." Reggie took Bell's arm and strolled away.

They wandered down to the little old church, "Makes you feel melancholy, sir, don't it?" Bell said. "Desolate, as you might say. As if people had got tired of believing in God."

Reggie looked at him a moment and went into the porch and tried the worm-eaten oak door. "We might have a look at the place," he said, and took out of his pocket a flat case like a housewife.

"Good Lord, sir, I wouldn't do that," Bell recoiled. "I mean to say-it's a church after all."

But Reggie was already picking the old lock. The door yielded and he went in. A dank and musty smell met them. The church was all but empty. Dim light fell on a shattered rood screen and stalls, and a bare stone altar. A tomb bore two cadaverous effigies. Reggie moved hither and thither prying into every corner, and came at last to a broken flight of stairs. "Oh, there's a crypt, is there," he muttered, and went down. "Hallo! Come on, Bell."

Superintendent Bell, following reluctantly, found him struggling with pieces of timber, relics of stall and bench, which held a door closed. "Give me a hand, man."

"I don't like it, sir, and that's the truth."

"Nor do I," Reggie panted, "not a bit," and dragged the last piece away and pulled the door open. He took out a torch and flashed the light on. They looked into a place supported on low round arches. The beam of the torch moved from coffin to mouldering coffin.

"Good God," Bell gasped, and gripped Reggie's arm.

Reggie drew him in. They came to the body of a man which had no coffin. It lay upon its face. Reggie bent over it, touching gently the back of the neck. "I thought so," he muttered, and turned the body over. Bell gave a stifled cry.

"Quite so, quite —" he sprang up and made a dash for the door. It was slammed in his face. He flung himself against it, and it yielded a little but held. A dull creaking and groaning told that the timbers were being set again in place. Together they charged the door and were beaten back "And that's that, Bell," said Reggie. He flashed his light round the crypt, and it fell again on the corpse. "You and me and the butler."

Bell's hand felt for him. "Mr. Fortune-Mr. Fortune-was he dead when he came here?"

"Oh Lord, yes. Sir Brian's quite a humane man. But business is business."

"Sir Brian?" Bell gasped.

"My dear chap," said Reggie irritably, "don't make conversation." He turned his torch on the grey oak of the door....

It was late in that grim afternoon before they had cut and kicked a hole in it, and Reggie's hand came through and felt for the timbers which held it closed. Twilight was falling when, dirty and reeking, they broke out of the church and made for the Hall.

Sir Brian-the new butler could not conceal his surprise at seeing them-Sir Brian had gone out in the big car. But the butler feared there must be some mistake. He understood that Sir Brian had seen the gentlemen and was to take them with him. Sir Brian had sent the gentlemen's car back to Southam. Sir Brian——

"Where's your telephone?" said Reggie.

The butler was afraid the telephone was out of order. He had been trying to get——

Reggie went to the receiver. There was no answer. Still listening, he looked at the connexions. A couple of inches of wire were cut out. Half an hour later two breathless men arrived at the village post office and shut themselves into the telephone call-box.

On the next day Lomas called at Mr. Fortune's house in Wimpole Street and was told that Mr. Fortune was in his bath. A parlourmaid with downcast eyes announced to him a few minutes later that if he would go up Mr. Fortune would be very glad to see him.

"Pardon me," said the pink cherubic face from the water. "I am not clean. I think I shall never be clean again."

"You look like a prawn," said Lomas.

"That's your unscientific mind. Have you got him?"

Lomas shook his head. "He has been seen in ten places at once. They have arrested a blameless bookmaker at Hull and an Irish cattle-dealer at Birkenhead. As usual. But we ought to have him in time."

"My fault entirely. He is an able fellow. I have underrated these business men, Lomas. My error. Occasionally one has a head. He has."

"These madmen often have."

Reggie wallowed in the water. "Mad? He's as sane as I am. He's been badly educated, that's all. That's the worst of business men. They're so ignorant. Just look at it. He killed Hugo by a knife thrust in the vertebrae at the base of the skull. It's a South American fashion, probably indigenous. When I found that wound in the body I was sure of the murderer. I had a notion before from the way he spoke about Hugo and the estate. Probably Hugo was bent over the table and the blow was struck without his knowledge. He would be dead in a moment. But Sir Brian saw that wouldn't do. Too uncommon a murder in England. So he smashed in the skull to make it look like an ordinary crime of violence. Thus ignorance is bliss. He never thought the death wasn't the right kind of death for that. Also it didn't occur to him that a man who is hit on the head hard is knocked down. He don't lay his head on the table to be hammered same like Hugo. I don't fancy Brian meant Mark to be hanged. Possibly he was going to manufacture evidence of burglary when he was interrupted by the butler. Anyhow the butler knew too much and had to be bought off. But I suppose the butler wouldn't stand Mark being hanged. When he found the trial was going dead against Mark he threatened. So he had to be killed too. Say by appointment in the park. Same injury in his body—a stab through the cervical vertebrae. And the corpse was neatly disposed of in the crypt."

"What in the world put you on to the crypt?"

"Well, Sir Brian was so anxious not to be interested in the place. And the place was so mighty convenient. And the butler had to be somewhere. Pure reasoning, Lomas, old thing. This is a very rational case all through."

"Rational! Will you tell me why Sir Brian came to stir us up about the butler and insisted Mark was innocent?"

"I told you he was an able man. He saw it would have looked very fishy if he didn't. Acting head of the family-he had to act. And also I fancy he liked Mark. If he could get the boy off, he would rather do it than not. And who could suspect the worthy fellow who was so straight and decent? All very rational."

"Very," said Lomas. "Especially the first murder. Why do you suppose he wanted to kill Hugo?"

"Well, you'd better look at his papers. He talked about Hugo as if he had a grudge against the way Hugo ran the estate. I wonder if he wanted to develop it-try for minerals perhaps-it's on the edge of the South Midland coal-field —and Hugo wouldn't have it."

"Good Gad!" Lomas said. "You're an ingenious fellow, Fortune. He had proposed to Hugo to try for coal, and Hugo turned it down."

Reggie emerged from the bath. "There you have it. He knew if Hugo was out of the way he could do what he wanted. If Mark or the old parson had the place, he could manage them. Very rational crime."

"Rational! Murder your cousin to make a coal mine!"

"Business men and business methods. Run away and catch him, Lomas, and hang him to encourage the others."

But in fact Lomas did not catch him. Some years afterwards Mrs. Fortune found her husband on the veranda of an hotel in Italy staring at a Spanish paper. "Don't dream, child," she said. "Run and dress."

"I'm seeing ghosts, Joan," said Mr. Fortune.

She looked over his shoulder. "Who is San Jacinto?"

"The last new South American republic. Here's His Excellency the President. *Né* Brian Carwell. Observe the smile."

CASE III

THE YOUNG DOCTOR

MR. REGINALD FORTUNE came into Superintendent Bell's room at Scotland Yard. "That was chocolate cream," he said placidly. "You'd better arrest the aunt."

The superintendent took up his telephone receiver and spoke into it fervently. You remember the unpleasant affair of the aunt and her niece's child.

" 'Oh, fat white woman that nobody loves,' " Mr. Fortune murmured. "Well, well. She's not wholesome, you know. Some little error in the ductless glands."

"She's for it," said Superintendent Bell with grim satisfaction. "That's a wicked woman, Mr. Fortune, and as clever as sin."

"Yes, quite unhealthy. A dull case, Bell." He yawned and wandered about the room and came to a stand by the desk. "What are these curios?" He pointed to a skeleton key and a pad of cotton-wool.

"The evidence in that young doctor's case, the Bloomsbury diamond burglary. Not worth keeping, I suppose. That was a bad business though. I was sorry for the lad. But it was a straight case. Did you read it, sir? Young fellow making a start, hard fight for it, on his beam ends, gets to know a man with a lot of valuable stuff in his rooms-and steals it. An impudent robbery too-but that's the usual way when a decent fellow goes wrong, he loses his head. Lead us not into temptation. That's the moral of Dr. Wilton's case. He's only thirty, he's a clever fellow, he ought to have done well, he's ruined himself-and if he'd had a hundred pounds in the bank he'd have run straight enough."

"A lot of crime is a natural product." Mr. Fortune repeated a favourite maxim of his. "I didn't read it, Bell. How did it go?" He sat down and lit a cigar.

"The trial was in this morning's papers, sir. Only a small affair. Dr. Horace Wilton came out of the army with a gratuity and a little money of his own. He set up as a specialist. You know the usual thing. His plate up with three or four others on a Harley Street house where he had a little consulting-room to himself. He lived in a Bloomsbury flat. Well, the patients didn't come. He wasn't known, he had no friends, and his money began to run out."

"Poor devil," Reggie nodded.

"A Dutch diamond merchant called Witt came to live in the flats. Wilton got to know him, prescribed for a cold or something. Witt took to the doctor, made friends, heard about his troubles, offered to get him a berth in the Dutch colonies, gave him two or three rough diamonds —a delicate way of giving him money, I suppose. Then one morning the valet-service flats they are-coming into Witt's rooms found him heavily asleep. He'd been chloroformed. There was that pad on his pillow."

Reggie took up the box in which the cotton-wool and the skeleton key lay.

"Don't shake it," said the superintendent. "Do you see those scraps of tobacco? That's important. The bureau in which Witt kept the diamonds he had with him had been forced open and the diamonds were gone. Witt sent for the police. Now you see that tobacco on the cotton-wool. The inspector spotted that. The cotton-wool must have been handled by a man who smoked that tobacco. Most likely carried it in the same pocket. Unusual stuff, isn't it? Well, the inspector remarked on that to Witt. Witt was horrified. You see it's South African tobacco. And he knew Wilton used the stuff. There was some spilt in the room, too."

"Have you got that?" said Reggie.

"No. I don't think it was produced. But our man saw it, and he's reliable. Then a Dutch journalist dropped in. He was just over in England. He'd called on Witt late the night before and couldn't make him hear. That surprised him because as he came up he'd seen some one coming out of Witt's rooms, some one who went into Wilton's. That was enough to act on. Wilton was arrested and his flat was searched. Tucked away in the window seat they found the diamonds and that skeleton key. He stood his trial yesterday, he made no defence but to swear that he knew nothing about it. The evidence was clear. Witt-he must be a soft-hearted old fellow-Witt tried to let him down as gently as he could and asked the judge to go easy with him. Old Borrowdale gave him five years. A stiff sentence, but the case itself would break the man's career, poor chap. A bad business, sir, isn't it? Impudent, ungrateful piece of thieving-but he might have been honest enough if he could have made a living at his job."

Mr. Fortune did not answer. He was looking at the key. He set it down, took up a magnifying glass, carried the box to the light and frowned over the cotton-wool.

"What's the matter with it, sir?"

"The key," Mr. Fortune mumbled, still studying the cotton-wool. "Why was the key made in Germany? Why does Dr. Horace Wilton of Harley Street and Bloomsbury use a skeleton key that was made in Solingen?"

"Well, sir, you can't tell how a man comes by that sort of stuff. It goes about from hand to hand, don't it?"

"Yes. Whose hand?" said Reggie. "And why does your local expert swear this is South African tobacco? There is a likeness. But this is that awful stuff they sell in Germany and call Rauch-tabak."

Bell was startled. "That's awkward, sir. German too, eh?"

"Well, you can buy Solingen goods outside Germany. And German tobacco, too. Say in Holland."

"I don't know what you're thinking, sir?"

"Oh, I think the tobacco was a little error. I think the tobacco ought not to have been there. But it was rather unlucky for Dr. Wilton your bright expert took it for his brand."

The superintendent looked uncomfortable. "Yes, sir, that's the sort of thing we don't want to happen. But after all the case didn't turn on the tobacco. There was the man who swore he saw Wilton leaving Witt's flat and the finding of the diamonds in Wilton's room. Without the tobacco the evidence was clear."

"I know. I said the tobacco was superfluous. That's why it interests me. Superfluous, not to say awkward. We know Wilton don't use Rauch-tabak. Yet there is Rauch-tabak on the chloroformed pad. Which suggests that some one else was on the job. Some fellow with a taste for German flavours. The sort of fellow who'd use a German key."

"There's not a sign of Wilton's having an accomplice," said Bell heavily. "But of course it's possible."

Mr. Fortune looked at him with affection. "Dear Bell," he said, "you must find the world very wonderful. No, I wouldn't look for an accomplice. But I think you might look for the diamond merchant and the journalist. I should like to ask them who smokes Rauch-tabak."

"There must be an investigation," Bell sighed. "I see that, sir. But I can't see that it will do the poor fellow any good. And it's bad for the department."

Reggie smiled upon him. "Historic picture of an official struggling with his humanity," he said. "Poor old Bell!"

At the end of that week Mr. Fortune was summoned to Scotland Yard. He found the chief of the Criminal Investigation Department in conference with Eddis, a man of law from the Home Office.

"Hallo! Life is real, life is earnest, isn't it, Lomas?" he smiled.

The Hon. Sidney Lomas put up an eyeglass and scowled at him. "You know, you're not a man of science, Fortune. You're an agitator. You ought to be bound over to keep the peace."

"I should call him a departmental nuisance," said Eddis gloomily.

"In returnin' thanks (one of your larger cigars would do me no harm, Lomas) I would only ask, where does it hurt you?"

"The Wilton case was a very satisfactory case till you meddled," said Eddis. "Also it was a *chose jugée* ."

"And now it's unjudged? How good for you!" Reggie chuckled. "How stimulating!"

"Now," said Lomas severely, "it's insane. It's a nightmare."

"Yes. Yes, I dare say that's what Dr. Wilton thinks," said Reggie gravely. "Well, how far have you got?"

"You were right about the tobacco, confound you. And the key. Both of German birth. And will you kindly tell me what that means?"

"My honourable friend's question," said Reggie, "should be addressed to Mynheer Witt or Mynheer Gerard. You know, this is like Alice in Wonderland. Sentence first, trial afterwards. Why didn't you look into the case before you tried it? Then you could have asked Witt and Gerard these little questions when you had them in the box. And very interesting too."

"We can't ask them now, at any rate. They've vanished. Witt left his flat on the day of the trial. Gerard left his hotel the same night. Both said they were going back to Amsterdam. And here's the Dutch police information. 'Your telegram of the 27th not understood. No men as described known in Amsterdam. Cannot trace arrivals.'"

"Well, well," said Reggie. "Our active and intelligent police force. The case has interest, hasn't it, Lomas, old thing?"

"What is it you want to suggest, Fortune?" Eddis looked at him keenly.

"I want to point out the evanescence of the evidence-the extraordinary evanescence of the evidence."

"That's agreed," Eddis nodded. "The whole thing is unsatisfactory. The tobacco, so far as it is evidence, turns out to be in favour of the prisoner. The only important witnesses for the prosecution disappear after the trial leaving suspicion of their status. But there remains the fact that the diamonds were found in the prisoner's room."

"Oh yes, some one put 'em there," Reggie smiled.

"Let's have it clear, Fortune," said the man of law. "Your suggestion is that the whole case against Wilton was manufactured by these men who have disappeared?"

"That is the provisional hypothesis. Because nothing else covers the facts. There were German materials used, and Wilton has nothing to do with Germany. The diamond merchant came to the flats where Wilton was already living and sought Wilton's acquaintance. The diamond merchant's friend popped up just in the nick of time to give indispensable evidence. And the moment Wilton is safe in penal servitude the pair of them vanish, and the only thing we can find out about them is that they aren't what they pretended to be. Well, the one hypothesis which fits all these facts is that these two fellows wanted to put Dr. Horace Wilton away. Any objection to that, Eddis?"

"There's only one objection-why? Your theory explains everything that happened, but leaves us without any reason why anything happened at all. That is, it's an explanation which makes the case more obscure than ever. We can understand why Wilton might have stolen diamonds. Nobody can understand why anyone should want to put him in prison."

"Oh my dear fellow! You're so legal. What you don't know isn't knowledge. You don't know why Wilton had to be put out of the way. No more do I. But——"

"No more did Wilton," said Eddis sharply. "He didn't suspect these fellows. His defence didn't suggest that he had any enemies. He only denied all knowledge of the theft, and his counsel argued that the real thief had used his rooms to hide the diamonds in because he was surprised and scared."

"Yes. That was pretty feeble, wasn't it? These lawyers, Eddis, these lawyers! A stodgy tribe."

"We do like evidence."

"Then why not use it? The man Witt was very interesting in the box. He said that in the kindness of his heart he had offered this ungrateful young doctor a job in the Dutch colonies. Quite a nice long way from England, Eddis. Wilton wouldn't take it. So Wilton had to be provided for otherwise."

Eddis looked at him thoughtfully. "I agree there's something in that. But why? We know all about Wilton. He's run quite straight till now-hospital career, military service, this private practice all straightforward and creditable. How should he have enemies who stick at nothing to get him out of the way? A man in a gang of criminals or revolutionaries is sometimes involved in a sham crime by the others to punish him, or for fear he should betray them. But that can't be Wilton's case. His life's all open and ordinary. I suppose a man might have private enemies who would use such a trick, though I don't know another case."

"Oh Lord, yes," said Lomas, "there was the Buckler affair. I always thought that was the motive in the Brendon murder."

Eddis frowned. "Well—as you say. But Wilton has no suspicion of a trumped-up case. He doesn't know he has enemies."

"No," said Reggie. "I rather think Wilton don't know what it is he knows. Suppose he blundered on some piece of awkward evidence about Mr. Witt or some of Mr. Witt's friends. He don't know it's dangerous—but they do."

"Men have been murdered in a case like that and never knew why they were killed," said Lomas.

"I dare say," Eddis cried. "It's all quite possible. But it's all in the air. I have nothing that I can act upon."

"Oh, I wouldn't say that," said Reggie. "You're so modest."

"Perhaps I am," Eddis shrugged. "But I can't recommend Wilton's sentence for revision on a provisional hypothesis."

"Revision be damned," Reggie cried. "I want him free."

Eddis stared at him. "But this is fantastic," he protested.

"Free and cleared. My God, think of the poor beggar in a convict gang because these rascals found him inconvenient. To reduce his sentence is only another wrong. He wants you to give him his life back."

"It is a hard case," Eddis sighed. "But what can I do? I can't clear the man's character. If we let him out now, he's a broken man."

"My dear fellow, I'm saying so," said Reggie mildly. "There's also another point. What is it Mr. Witt's up to that's so important? I could bear to know that."

"That's not my job," said Eddis with relief. "But you're still in the air, Fortune. What do you want to do? I must take some action."

"And that's very painful to any good official. I sympathize with you. Lomas sympathizes with you more, don't you, Lomas, old thing? And I'm not sure that you can do any good." Mr. Fortune relapsed into cigar smoke and meditation.

"You're very helpful," said Eddis.

"The fact is, all the evidence against the man has gone phut," said Lomas. "It's deuced awkward, but we have to face it. Better let him out, Eddis."

Eddis gasped. "My dear Lomas! I really can't follow you. The only evidence which is proved false is the tobacco, which wasn't crucial. The rest is open to suspicion, but we can't say it's false, and it satisfied the judge and jury. It's unprecedented to reduce the sentence to nothing in such a case."

"I'm not thinking of your troubles," said Lomas. "I want to know what Mr. Witt has up his sleeve."

Reggie came out of his smoke. "Let Wilton out—have him watched—and see what Witt and Co. get up to. Well, that's one way. But it's a gamble."

"It's also out of the question," Eddis announced.

Reggie turned on him. "What exactly are you for, Eddis?" he said. "What is the object of your blessed existence?"

Eddis remarked coldly that it was not necessary to lose one's temper.

"No. No, I'm not cross with you, but you puzzle my simple mind. I thought your job was to see justice done. Well, get on with it."

"If you'll be so very good as to say what you suggest," said Eddis, flushing.

"You'll say it's unprecedented. Well, well. This is my little notion. Tell the defence about the tobacco and say that that offers a ground for carrying the case to the Court of Appeal. Then let it get into the papers that there's a doubt about the conviction, probability of the Wilton case being tried again, and so on. Something rather pompous and mysterious to set the papers going strong about Wilton." He smiled at Lomas. "I think we could wangle that?"

"I have known it done," said Lomas.

"Good heavens, I couldn't have any dealings with the press," Eddis cried.

"Bless your sweet innocence. We'll manage it. It don't matter what the papers say so long as they say a lot. That'll wake up Witt and Co., and we'll see what happens."

Eddis looked horrified and bewildered. "I think it is clear the defence should be advised of the flaw discovered in the evidence in order that the conviction may be reviewed by the Court of Appeal," he said solemnly. "But of course I—I couldn't sanction anything more."

"That's all right, my dear fellow," Lomas smiled "Nobody sanctions these things. Nobody does them. They only happen." And Eddis was got rid of.

"My country, oh my country!" Reggie groaned. "That's the kind of man that governs England."

A day or two later saw Mr. Fortune shivering on an April morning outside Princetown prison. He announced to the governor that he wanted to get to know Dr. Wilton.

"I don't think you'll make much of him," the governor shook his head. "The man seems stupefied. Of course a fellow who has been in a good position often is so when he comes here. Wilton's taking it very hard. When we told him there was a flaw in the evidence and he could appeal against his sentence, he showed no interest. He was sullen and sour as he has been all the time. All he would say was 'What's the good? You've done for me.' "

"Poor devil," Reggie sighed.

"It may be." The governor looked dubious. "No one can judge a man's character on his first days in prison. But I've known men who gave me a good deal more reason to believe them innocent."

Dr. Wilton was brought in, a shred of a man in his prison clothes. A haggard face glowered at Reggie. "My name's Fortune, Dr. Wilton," Reggie held out his hand. It was ignored. "I come from Scotland Yard. I found the mistake which had been made about the tobacco. It made me very interested in your case. I feel sure we don't know the truth of it. If you can help me to that it's going to help you." He waited.

"The police can't help me," said Wilton. "I'm not going to say anything."

"My dear chap, I know that was a bad blunder. But there's more than that wants looking into. If you'll give us a chance we might be able to clear up the whole case and set you on your feet again. That's what I'm here for."

And Wilton laughed. "No thanks," he said unpleasantly.

"Just think of it. I can't do you any harm. I'm looking for the truth. I'm on your side. What I want to know is, have you got any enemies? Anyone who might like to damage you? Anybody who wanted to put you out of the way?"

"Only the police," said Wilton.

"Oh, my dear chap!" Reggie brushed that away. "Did anything strange ever happen to you before this charge?"

"What?" Wilton flushed. "Oh, I see. I'm an old criminal, am I? Better look for my previous convictions. Or you can invent 'em. Quite easy."

"My dear chap, what good can this do you?" said Reggie sadly. "The police didn't invent this charge. Your friend Mr. Witt made it. Do you know anything about Mr. Witt? Did it ever occur to you he wanted you off the scene-in the Dutch colonies-or in prison?"

"I've nothing against Witt," said Wilton.

"Oh, my dear fellow! How did the diamonds get in your room?"

"Yes, how did they?" said Wilton savagely. "Ask your police inspector. The man who said that was my tobacco. You're a policeman. You know how these jobs are done."

"I wish I did," Reggie sighed. "If I did I dare say you wouldn't be here."

But he could get no more out of Dr. Wilton. He went away sorrowful. He had not recovered his spirits when he sought Lomas next morning. Lomas was brisk. "You're the man I want. What's the convict's theory of it?"

Reggie shook his head. "Lomas, old thing, do I ever seem a little vain of my personal charm? The sort of fellow who thinks fellows can't resist him?"

"Nothing offensive, Fortune. A little childlike, perhaps. You do admire yourself, don't you?"

"Quoth the raven 'Nevermore.' When you find me feeling fascinating again, kindly murmur the name Wilton. I didn't fascinate him. Not one little damn. He was impossible."

"You surprise me," said Lomas gravely. "Nothing out of him at all?"

"Too much, too much," Reggie sighed. "Sullen, insolent, stupid-that was our young doctor, poor devil. It was the wicked police that did him in, a put-up job by the force, the inspector hid the diamonds in his room to spite him. Such was Dr. Horace Wilton, the common, silly criminal to the life. It means nothing, of course. The poor beggar's dazed. Like a child kicking the naughty chair that he fell over."

"I'm not so sure," said Lomas. "The inspector has shot himself, Fortune. We had him up here, you know, to inquire into the case. He was nervous and confused. He went back home and committed suicide." Reggie Fortune huddled himself together in his chair. "Nothing against the man before. There's only this question of the tobacco against him now. But it looks ugly, doesn't it?"

"We know he said the tobacco was what it isn't. If that made him kill himself he was too conscientious for a policeman, poor beggar. Why does it look ugly, Lomas? I think it's pitiful. My God, if we all shot ourselves when we made mistakes, there would be vacancies in the force. Poor Wilton said the inspector put the diamonds in his room. But that's crazy."

"It's all crazy. You are a little confused yourself, Fortune. You say it's preposterous for the man to shoot himself merely because he made a mistake, and equally preposterous to suppose he had any other reason."

"Poor beggar, poor beggar," Reggie murmured. "No, Lomas, I'm not confused. I'm only angry. Wilton's not guilty and your inspector's not guilty. And one's in prison and one's dead, and we call ourselves policemen. Shutting the stable door after the horse's stolen, that's a policeman's job. But great heavens, we don't even shut the door."

Lomas shook his head. "Not only angry, I fear, but rattled. My dear Fortune, what can we do?"

"Witt hasn't shown his hand?"

"Not unless he had a hand in the inspector's suicide."

"I suppose it was suicide?"

"Well, you'd better look at the body. The evidence is good enough."

"Nothing in the papers?"

Lomas stared at him. "Columns of course. All quite futile. You didn't expect evidence in the papers, did you?"

"You never know, you know. You don't put a proper value on the Press, Lomas."

It has been remarked of Mr. Fortune that when he is interested he will do everything himself. This is considered by professional critics a weakness. Yet in this case of the young doctor, where he was continually occupied with details, he seems to have kept a clear head for strategy.

He went to see the inspector's body in the mortuary. He came out in gloomy thought.

"Satisfied, sir?" said Superintendent Bell, who escorted him.

Reggie stopped and stared at him. "Oh, Peter, what a word!" he muttered. "Satisfied! No, Bell, not satisfied. Only infuriated. He killed himself all right, poor beggar. One more victim for Witt and Company."

"What's the next move, sir?"

"Goodbye," said Mr. Fortune. "I'm going home to read the papers."

With all the London papers which had appeared since the news that there was a doubt about the justice of Wilton's conviction had been given them, he shut himself into his study. Most of them had taken the hint that there was a mystery in the case and made a lot of it. The more rational were content to tell the story in detail, pointing out the incongruity of such a man as Wilton and the crime. The more fatuous put out wild inventions as to the theories held by the police. But there was general sympathy with Dr. Wilton, a general readiness to expect that he would be cleared. He had a good press-except for the "Daily Watchman."

The "Daily Watchman" began in the same strain as the rest of the sillier papers, taking Wilton's innocence for granted, and devising crazy explanations of the burglary. But on the third day it burst into a different tune. Under a full-page headline "The Wilton Scandal," its readers were warned against the manufactured agitation to release the man Wilton. It was a trick of politicians and civil servants and intellectuals to prevent the punishment of a rascally criminal. It was another case of one law for the rich and another for the poor. It was a corrupt job to save a scoundrel who had friends in high places. It was, in fine, all sorts of iniquity, and the British people must rise in their might and keep the wicked Wilton in gaol if they did not want burglars calling every night.

Mr. Fortune went to sup at that one of his clubs used by certain journalists. There he sought and at last found Simon Winterbottom, the queerest mixture of scholarship, slang, and backstairs gossip to be found in London. "Winter," said he, having stayed the man with flagons, "who runs the 'Daily Watchman'?"

"My God!" Winterbottom was much affected. "Are you well, Reginald? Are you quite well? It's the wonkiest print on the market. All newspapers are run by madmen, but the 'Watchman' merely dithers."

"You said 'on the market,'" Reggie repeated. "Corrupt?"

"Well, naturally. Too balmy to live honest. Why this moral fervour, Reginald? I know you're officially a guardian of virtue, but you mustn't let it weigh on your mind."

"I want to know why the 'Watchman' changed sides on the Wilton case."

Winterbottom grinned. "That was a giddy stunt, wasn't it? The complete Gadarene. I don't know, Reginald. Why ask for reasons? Let twenty pass and stone the twenty-first, loving not, hating not, just choosing so."

"I wonder," Reggie murmured. "It's the change of mind. The sudden change of mind. This is rather a bad business, Winter."

"Oh, simian," Winterbottom agreed. His comical face was working. "You are taking it hard, Reginald."

"I'm thinking of that poor devil Wilton. Who got at the Watchman, old thing? I could bear to know."

On the next day but one Mr. Fortune received a letter.

Dear R. —

The greaser Kemp who owns the "Watchman" came in one bright day, cancelled all instructions on the Wilton case and dictated the new line. No known cause for the rash act. It leaks from his wretched intimates that Kemp has a new pal, one Kuyper, a ruffian said by some to be a Hun, certainly a City mushroom. This seems highly irrelevant. You must not expect Kemp to be rational even in his vices. Sorry.

S. W.

Mr. Fortune went into the city and consumed turtle soup and oyster patties with Tommy Owen, the young son of an ancient firm of stockbrokers. When they were back again in the dungeon which is Tommy's office, "Thomas, do you know anything of one Kuyper?" he said.

"Wrong number, old bean," Tommy Owen shook his round head. "Not in my department. International finance is Mr. Julius Kuyper's line."

Reggie smiled. It is the foible of Tommy Owen to profess ignorance. "Big business?" he said.

"Not so much big business as queer business. Mr. Julius Kuyper blew into London some months ago. Yes, January. He is said to be negotiating deals in Russian mining properties."

"Sounds like selling gold bricks."

"Well, not in my department," said Tommy Owen again. "There's some money somewhere. Mr. Kuyper does the thing in style. He's thick with some fellows who don't go where money isn't. In point of fact, old dear, I've rather wondered about Mr. Kuyper. Do you know anything?"

"Nothing that fits, Tommy. What does he want in London?"

"Search me," said Tommy Owen. "I say, Fortune, when Russia went pop some blokes must have laid their hands on a lot of good stuff. I suppose you fellows at Scotland Yard know where it's gone?"

"I wonder if your friend Kuyper's been dealing in jewels."

Tommy Owen looked wary. "Don't that fit, old bean? There's a blighter that's been busy with brother Kuyper blossomed out with a rare old black pearl in his tiepin. They used to tell me the good black pearls went to Russia."

"What is Kuyper? A Hun?"

"I wouldn't bet on it. He might be anything. Lean beggar, oldish, trim little beard, very well groomed, talks English well, says he's a Dutchman. You could see him yourself. He has offices in that ghastly new block in Mawdleyn Lane."

"Thanks very much, Thomas," said Mr. Fortune.

"Oh, not a bit. Sorry I don't know anything about the blighter," said Tommy Owen, and Mr. Fortune laughed.

As a taxi took him home to Wimpole Street he considered his evidence. The mysterious Kuyper said he was Dutch. The vanished Witt also said he was Dutch. Kuyper said he was selling Russian jewels. Witt also dealt in jewels. Mr. Fortune went home and telephoned to Lomas that Julius Kuyper of Mawdleyn Lane should be watched, and by men of experience.

Even over the telephone the voice of Lomas expressed surprise. "Kuyper?" it repeated. "What is the reference, Fortune? The Wilton case. Quite so. You did say Julius Kuyper? But he's political. He's a Bolshevik."

Reggie also felt some surprise but he did not show it.

"Some of your men who've moved in good criminal society," he said firmly. "Rush it, old thing."

After breakfast on the next day but one he was going to the telephone to talk to Lomas when the thing rang at him. "Is that Fortune?" said Lomas's voice. "Speaking? The great Mr. Fortune! I looks towards you, Reginald. I likewise bows. Come right on."

Mr. Fortune found Lomas with Superintendent Bell. They lay back in their chairs and looked at him. Lomas started up, came to him and walked round him, eyeglass up.

"What is this?" said Mr. Fortune. "Dumb crambo?"

"Admiration," Lomas sighed. "Reverence. Awe. How do you do these things, Fortune? You look only human, not to say childlike. Yet you have us all beat. You arrive while we're still looking for the way."

"I wouldn't have said it was a case for Mr. Fortune, either," said Bell.

"No flowers, by request. Don't be an owl, Lomas. Who is Kuyper?"

Lomas sat down again. "I hoped you were going to tell us that," he said. "What in the world made you go for Kuyper?"

"He calls himself Dutch and so did Witt. He deals in jewels and so did Witt. And I fancy he set the 'Daily Watchman' howling that Wilton must stay in prison."

"And if you will kindly make sense of that for me I shall be obliged," said Lomas.

"It doesn't make sense. I know that. Hang it all, you must do something for yourselves. Justify your existence, Lomas. Who is Kuyper?"

"The political branch have had their eye on him for some time. He's been selling off Russian jewels. They believe he's a Bolshevik."

"That don't help us," Reggie murmured.

"No. The connexion of Wilton with Bolshevism isn't what you'd call obvious. I did think you were hunting the wild, wild goose, Reginald. All my apologies. None of our men recognized Kuyper. But one of them did recognize Mr. Witt. Mr. Witt is now something in Kuyper's office. Marvellous, Reginald. How do you do it?"

"My head," said Reggie Fortune. "Oh, my head! Kuyper's a Bolshevik agent and Kuyper employs a man to put Wilton out of the way. It's a bad dream."

"Yes, it's not plausible. Not one of your more lucid cases, Fortune."

"I had thought," said Bell diffidently, "if Dr. Wilton happened to get to know of some Bolshevik plot, Mr. Fortune, they would be wanting to put him out."

"They would—in a novel," Reggie shook his head. "But hang it all, Wilton don't know that he ever knew anything."

"P'r'aps he's a bit of a Bolshevik himself, sir," said Bell.

Lomas laughed. "Bell has a turn for melodrama."

"Yes. Yes, there is a lot of melodrama in the world. But somehow I don't fancy Kuyper, Witt and Co. play it. I think I'll go and have a little talk with the firm."

"You?" Lomas stared at him.

"Not alone, I reckon, sir." Bell stood up.

"Well, you come and chaperon me. Yes, I want to look at 'em, Lomas. Wilton's a medical man, you know. I want to see the patients, too."

"You can try it," Lomas said dubiously. "You realize we have nothing definite against Witt, and nothing at all against Kuyper. And I'm not sure that Kuyper hasn't smelt a rat. He's been staying at the Olympian. He was there on Tuesday night, but last night our men lost him."

"Come on, Bell," said Mr. Fortune.

Outside the big new block in Mawdlyn Lane Superintendent Bell stopped a moment and looked round. A man crossed the road and made a sign as he vanished into a doorway.

"He's in, sir," Bell said, and they went up to the offices of Mr. Julius Kuyper.

A pert young woman received them. They wanted to see Mr. Kuyper? By appointment? Oh, Mr. Kuyper never saw anyone except by appointment.

"He'll see me," said Bell, and gave her a card. She looked him over impudently and vanished. Another young woman peered round the glass screen at them.

"Sorry." The first young woman came briskly back. "Mr. Kuyper's not in. Better write and ask for an appointment."

"That won't do. Who is in?" said Bell heavily.

"Don't you bully me!" she cried.

"You don't want to get into trouble, do you?" Bell frowned down at her. "You go in there and say Superintendent Bell is waiting to see Mr. Witt."

"We haven't got any Mr. Witt."

"You do as you're told."

She went. She was gone a long time. A murmur of voices was audible. She came out again, looking flustered. "Well, what about it?" said Bell.

"I don't know anything about it," she said. A door slammed, a bell rang. She made a nervous exclamation and turned to answer it. Bell went first and Reggie on his heels.

In the inner room an oldish man stood smoothing his hair. He was flushed and at the sight of Bell he cried out: "But you intrude, sir."

"Ah, here's our old friend, Mr. Witt," Bell smiled. "I should——"

"There is some mistake. You are wrong, sir. What is your name? Mr. Superintendent—my name is Siegel."

"I dare say it is. Then why did you call yourself Witt?"

"I do not know what you mean."

"I don't forget faces. I should know you anywhere. You're the Mr. Witt who prosecuted Dr. Horace Wilton. Come, come, the game's up now."

"What do you mean by that, sir?"

"Time to tell the truth," said Reggie sweetly, "time you began to think of yourself, isn't it? We know all about the evidence in the Wilton burglary. Why did you do it, Mr. Witt? It wasn't safe, you know."

"What do you want?"

"Well, where's your friend Mr. Kuyper? We had better have him in."

"Mr. Kuyper has gone out, sir."

Reggie laughed. "Oh, I don't think so. You're not doing yourself justice. I don't suppose you wanted to trap Dr. Wilton. You'd better consider your position. What is Mr. Kuyper's little game with you?"

Mr. Witt looked nervously round the room. "You-you mustn't —I mean we can't talk here," he said. "The girls will be listening."

"Oh, send the girls out to tea," said Bell.

"No. I can't do that. I had rather come with you, Mr. Superintendent. I would rather indeed."

"Come on then."

Mr. Witt, who was shaking with nervous fear, caught up his hat and coat. The farther door of the room was flung open. Two pistol shots were fired. As Reggie sprang at the door it was slammed in his face and locked. Mr. Witt went down in a heap. Bell dashed through the outer office into the corridor. Reggie knelt by Mr. Witt.

"Kuyper," Mr. Witt gasped. "Kuyper."

"I know. I know. We'll get him yet. Where's he gone?"

"His yacht," Mr. Witt gasped. "Yacht at Gravesend. He had it ready." He groaned and writhed. He was hit in the shoulder and stomach.

Reggie did what he could for the man, and went to the telephone. He had finished demanding an ambulance when Bell came back breathless, with policemen in uniform at his heels.

"The swine," Bell gasped. "He's off, sir. Must have gone down the other staircase into Bull Court. We had a man there but he wouldn't know there was anything up, he'd only follow. Pray God he don't lose him. They lost him last night."

"Send these girls away," said Mr. Fortune. "Let the constables keep the door. I want to use the telephone." And when the ambulance had come and taken Mr. Witt, happily unconscious at last, to hospital, he was still talking into the telephone. "Is that clear?" he concluded. "All right. Goodbye." He hung up the receiver. "Come on, Bell. It's Gravesend now. This is our busy day."

"Gravesend?" The superintendent stared.

But it was into a teashop that Reggie plunged when they reached the street. He came out with large paper bags just as a big car turned painfully into Mawdleyn Lane. "Good man," he smiled upon the chauffeur. "Gravesend police station. And let her out when you can." With his mouth full he expounded to Superintendent Bell his theory of the evasion of Mr. Kuyper.

As the car drew up in Gravesend a man in plain clothes came out of the police station. "Scotland Yard, sir?" Bell pulled a card out. "Inspector's down on the beach now. I was to take you to him."

By the pier the inspector was waiting. He hurried up to their car. "Got him?" said Bell.

"He's off. You didn't give us much time. But he's been here. A man answering to your description hired a motor yacht-cutter with auxiliary engine-six weeks ago. It was rather noticed, being an unusual time of year to start yachting. He's been down odd times and slept aboard. He seems to have slept aboard last night. I can't find anyone who's seen him here to-day. But there's a longshoreman swears he saw a Tilbury boat go alongside the *Cyrilla* —that's his yacht —a while since, and the *Cyrilla's* away."

"Have you got a fast boat ready for us?"

"At the pier head, sir. Motor launch."

"Good work," Reggie smiled. And they hurried on board.

"What's the job, sir?" The captain of the launch touched his cap.

45

"Dig out after the *Cyrilla*. You know her, don't you?"

"I do so. But I reckon she ain't in sight. What's the course?"

"Down stream. She'll be making for the Dutch coast. Are you good for a long run?"

"Surely. And I reckon it will be a long run. She's fast, is *Cyrilla*. Wind her up, Jim," and the launch began to throb through the water.

Mr. Fortune retired under the hood and lit his pipe, and Bell followed him. "He's smart, isn't he, sir, our Mr. Kuyper? His yacht at Gravesend and he comes down by Tilbury. That's neat work."

"Don't rub it in, Bell. I know I ought to have thought of Tilbury."

Bell stared at him. "Good Lord, Mr. Fortune, I'm not blaming you, sir."

"I am," said Reggie. "It's an untidy case, Bell. Well, well. I wonder if I've missed anything more?"

"I don't know what you've missed, sir. I know I wouldn't like to be on the run if you were after me."

Reggie looked at the large, man with a gleam of amusement. "It would be rather joyful, Bell," he chuckled, and was solemn again. "No. I am not happy. *Je n'ai pas de courage*. I want Mr. Kuyper."

It was a grey day. The Essex flats lay dim and sombre. The heights on the southern shore were blurred. Yet they could see far out to the Nore. An east wind was whipping the flood tide into tiny waves, through which the launch clove, making, after the manner of her kind, a great show of speed, leaving the tramps that chunked outward bound as though they lay at anchor.

"Do you see her yet?" Reggie asked the captain.

"Maybe that's her," he pointed to a dim line on the horizon beyond the lightship, a sailless mast, if it was anything. "Maybe not." He spat over the side.

"Are you gaining on her?"

"I reckon we're coming up, sir."

"What's that thing doing?" Reggie pointed to a long low black craft near the Nore.

"Destroyer, sir. Engines stopped."

"Run down to her, will you? How does one address the Navy, Bell? I feel shy. Ask him if he's the duty destroyer of the Nore Command, will you?"

"Good Lord, sir," said Bell.

The captain of the launch hailed. "Duty destroyer, sir?"

"Aye, aye. Scotland Yard launch? Come alongside."

"Thank God for the Navy, as the soldier said," Mr. Fortune murmured. "Perhaps it will be warmer on board her."

"I say, sir, did you order a destroyer out?"

"Oh, I asked Lomas to turn out the Navy. I thought we might want 'em."

Superintendent Bell gazed at him. "And you say you forget things," he said. "Witt's shot and all in a minute you have all this in your head."

They climbed a most unpleasant ladder. A young lieutenant received them. "You gentlemen got a job of work for us?"

"A motor yacht, cutter rig, name *Cyrilla*, left Gravesend an hour or two ago, probably making for the Dutch coast. There's a man on board that's badly wanted."

"Can do," the lieutenant smiled and ran up to the bridge. "Starboard five. Half ahead both." He spoke into a voice pipe. "You'd better come up here," he called to them. "We'll whack her up as we go."

The destroyer began to quiver gently to the purr of the turbines. Reggie cowered under the wind screen. The speed grew and grew and the destroyer sat down on her stern and on either side white waves rushed from the high sharp bow. "Who is your friend on the yacht?" the lieutenant smiled.

"His last is attempted murder. But that was only this morning."

"You fellows don't lose much time," said the lieutenant with more respect. "You seem to want him bad."

"I could bear to see him," said Reggie. "He interests me as a medical man."

"Medical?" the lieutenant stared at him.

"Quite a lot of crime is medical," said Reggie.

The lieutenant gave it up and again asked for more speed and began to use his binoculars. "There's a cutter rig," he pointed at something invisible. "Not under sail. Laying a course for Flushing. That's good enough, what?"

The destroyer came up fast. A white hull was revealed to the naked eye. The lieutenant spoke to his signalman and flags fluttered above the bridge. "Not answered. D'ye think your friend'll put up a scrap?"

"I dare say he will, if his crew will stand for it."

"Praise God," said the lieutenant. "Will they have any arms?"

"Pistols, likely," said Bell.

"Well! She is *Cyrilla* ." He picked up a megaphone and roared through it. "The cutter! *Cyrilla!* Stop your engine!"

There was some movement on the yacht's deck. She did stop her engine or slow. A shot was heard. She started her engine again and again stopped. A man ran aft and held up his hand. The destroyer drew abeam and the lieutenant said what occurred to him of yachts which did not obey Navy signals. There was no answer. A little knot of men on the *Cyrilla* gazed at the destroyer.

"You fellows going aboard her? Got guns? I'll give you an armed boat's crew."

Behind the destroyer's sub-lieutenant Bell and Reggie came to the yacht's deck. "Where's the captain? Don't you know enough to read signals?" Thus the sub-lieutenant began.

"Where's Mr. Kuyper?" said Bell.

"We didn't understand your signals, sir." The captain licked his lips. "Don't know anything about a Mr. Kuyper. We've got a Mr. Hotten, a Dutch gentleman. He's my owner, as you might say."

"Where is he?"

"Down the engine-room. It was him fired at the engineer to make him start her up again when I 'ad stopped. I laid him out with a spanner."

"Bring him up," Bell said.

A slim spruce body was laid on the deck, precisely the Julius Kuyper of Tommy Owen's description. Reggie knelt down beside him.

"He ain't dead, is he?" said the yacht's captain anxiously.

But the stertorous breath of Mr. Kuyper could be heard. "My only aunt," Reggie muttered.

"What's the matter, sir?"

"Man hasn't got a heart. This is very unusual. Good Lord! Heart well over on the right side. Heterotaxy very marked. Quite unusual. Ah! That's more to the point. He's had an operation on the thyroid gland. Yes. Just so." He smiled happily.

"What was that word you said, sir?"

"Heterotaxy? Oh, it only means he's got his things all over on the wrong side."

"Then I know him!" Bell cried. "I thought I knew the look of him, as old as he is now. It's Lawton, sir, Lawton of the big bank frauds. He went off with fifty thousand or more. Before your time, but you must have heard of it. Did a clear getaway."

"And that's that," said Reggie. "Now we know."

* * * * * *

Some days afterwards the Hon. Sidney Lomas called on Mr. Fortune, who was at the moment making a modest supper of devilled sole. "Did you clear it up?" he said.

"Try that champagne. It's young but has distinction. Oh yes. Dr. Wilton quite agrees with me. A faulty thyroid gland is the root of the trouble."

"I don't want to hear about Mr. Kuyper Lawton's diseases. I——"

"My dear fellow! But that is the whole case. Mr. Kuyper-Lawton is undoubtedly a man of great ability. But there was always a cachexis of the thyroid gland. This caused a certain mental instability. Unsound judgment. Violence of temper. It's quite common."

"Is it though?" said Lomas. "And why was he violent to poor Wilton?"

"Well, Lawton got clean away after his bank frauds, as you know——"

"I know all about Lawton. He lived on the plunder in Holland as Adrian Hotten and flourished till the war. Then he lost most of his money backing Germany to win. In the end of 1917 he went off to Russia. This year he turned up in London as Julius Kuyper, talking about Russian finance and selling Russian jewels."

"Quite so. Well, in February he was in a motor accident in Cavendish Square. A lorry hit his car and he was thrown out and stunned. The unfortunate Wilton was passing and gave him first-aid, and discovered that his heart was on the wrong side. He came to under Wilton's hands. I suppose Wilton showed a little too much interest. Anyhow, Mr. Kuyper saw that the malformation which would identify him with Lawton of the bank frauds was known to the young doctor. Well, he kept his head then. He was very grateful. He asked for Wilton's card. And Wilton never heard any more of him. But Wilton was interested in this striking case of heterotaxy. He noted the number of the car, found the garage from which it was hired and went round to ask who the man was. They wouldn't tell him, but the chauffeur, I suppose, told Mr. Kuyper the doctor was asking after him. He sent Witt to take a flat over Wilton's and find out what Wilton was up to. I take it Mr. Kuyper was doing mighty good business in London and didn't want to run away. He needn't have bothered-but that's the man all over, brilliantly ingenious and no judgment. That thyroid of his! Wilton had come to know the local detective-inspector, that poor chap who committed suicide. I'm mighty sorry for that fellow, Lomas. He was so keen against Wilton because he was afraid of not doing his duty when he liked the man-and then he found he'd blundered into giving false evidence against his friend. I don't wonder he chose to die."

"Conscience makes fools of us all," said Lomas.

"Yes. Yes. Poor beggar. And no wonder Wilton was bitter against him. Well, Kuyper decided that Wilton with his curiosity and his friend in the police wasn't safe at large. First they tried to ship him out of the country and he wouldn't go. So they put up the burglary. I suppose Witt or Witt's friend the sham Dutch journalist is a Hun. That accounts for the Rauch-tabak and the German keys."

"Lawton-Kuyper has done a lot of business with Germany himself."

"Yes. He ought to have been on the great General Staff. The right type of mind. One of our native Prussians. An able man —a very able man. If his thyroid had been healthy!"

CASE IV

THE MAGIC STONE

A NIGHTINGALE began to sing in the limes. Mr. Fortune smiled through his cigar smoke at the moon and slid lower into his chair. In the silver light his garden was a wonderland. He could see fairies dancing on the lawn. The fine odour of the cigar was glorified by the mingled fragrance of the night, the spicy scent of the lime flowers borne on a wind which came from the river over meadowsweet and hay. The music of the nightingale was heard through the soft murmur of the weir stream.

The head of the Criminal Investigation Department was arguing that the case of the Town Clerk of Barchester offered an example of the abuse of the simple poisons in married life.

Mr. Reginald Fortune, though his chief adviser, said no word.

The head of the Criminal Investigation Department came at last to an end. "That's the case, then." He stood up and knocked over his coffee cup: a tinkling clatter, a profound silence and then only the murmur of the water. The nightingale was gone. "Well, Fortune?"

Mr. Fortune sighed and raised himself. "Dear me, Lomas," he said sadly, "why don't you find something to do?"

The Hon. Sidney Lomas suffered from a sense of wrong and said so. It was a difficult and complex case and had given him much anxiety and he wanted Fortune's advice and———

"She did him in all right," said Reggie Fortune succinctly, "and you'll never find a jury to hang her. Why don't you bring me something interesting?"

Lomas then complained of him, pointing out that a policeman's life was not a happy one, that he did not arrange or even choose the crimes of his country. "Interesting? Good Gad, do you suppose I am interested in this female Bluebeard? I know my job's not interesting. Work's work."

"And eggs is eggs. You have no soul, Lomas." Reggie Fortune stood up. "Come and have a drink." He led the way from the dim veranda into his study and switched on the light. "Now that," he pointed to a pale purple fluid, "that is a romantic liqueur: it feels just like a ghost story: I brought it back from the Pyrenees."

"Whisky," said Lomas morosely.

"My dear chap, are we down-hearted?"

"You should go to Scotland Yard, Fortune." Lomas clung to his grievance. "Perhaps you would find it interesting. What do you think they brought me this afternoon? Some poor devil had an epileptic fit in the British Museum."

"Well, well"—Reggie Fortune sipped his purple liqueur—"the British Museum has made me feel queer. But not epileptic. On the contrary. Sprightly fellow. This is a nice story. Go on Lomas."

"That's all," Lomas snapped. "Interesting, isn't it?"

"Then why Scotland Yard? You're not an hospital for nervous diseases. Or are you, Lomas?"

"I wonder," said Lomas bitterly. "Why Scotland Yard? Just so. Why? Because they've lost an infernal pebble in the fray. And will I find it for them please? Most interesting case."

Reggie Fortune took another cigar and composed himself for comfort. "Begin at the beginning," he advised, "and relate all facts without passion or recrimination."

"There are no facts, confound you. It was in the Ethnological Gallery of the British Museum-where nobody ever goes. Some fellow did go and had a fit. He broke one of the glass cases in his convulsions. They picked him up and he came round. He was very apologetic, left them a fiver to pay for the glass and an address in New York. He was an American doing Europe and just off to France with his family. When they looked over the case afterwards they found one of the stones in it was gone. The epilept couldn't have taken it, poor devil. Anybody who was in the gallery might have pocketed it in the confusion. Most likely a child. The thing is only a pebble with some paint on it. A pundit from the Museum came to me with his hair on end and wanted me to sift London for it. I asked him what it was worth and he couldn't tell me.

49

Only an anthropologist would want the thing, he said. It seems an acquired taste. I haven't acquired it. I told him this was my busy day."

Reggie Fortune smiled benignly. "But this is art," he said. "This is alluring, Lomas. Have you cabled to New York?"

"Have I——?" Lomas stopped his whisky on the way to his mouth. "No, Fortune, I have not cabled New York. Nor have I sent for the military. The British Museum is still without a garrison."

"Well, you know, this gentleman with the fit may be a collector."

"Oh, Lord, no. It was a real fit. No deception. They had a doctor to him."

Reggie Fortune was much affected. "There speaks the great heart of the people. The doctor always knows! I love your simple faith, Lomas. It cheers me. But I'm a doctor myself. My dear chap, has no one ever murmured into the innocence of Scotland Yard that a fit can be faked?"

"I dare say I am credulous," said Lomas. "But I draw the line somewhere. If you ask me to believe that a fellow shammed epilepsy, cut himself and spent a fiver to pick up a pebble, I draw it there."

"That's the worst of credulity. It's always sceptical in the wrong place. What was this pebble like?"

Lomas reached for a writing-pad and drew the likeness of a fat cigar, upon which parallel to each other were two zigzag lines. "A greenish bit of stone, with those marks in red. That's the Museum man's description. If it had been old, which it isn't, it would have been a *galet coloré*. And if it had come from Australia, which it didn't, it would have been a chu-chu something——"

"Churinga."

"That's the word. The pundit from the Museum says it came from Borneo. They don't know what the marks mean, but the thing is a sort of mascot in Borneo: a high-class insurance policy. The fellow who holds it can't die. So the simple Bornese don't part with their pebbles easily. There isn't another known in Europe. That's where it hurts the Museum pundit. He says it's priceless. I told him marbles were selling thirty a penny. Nice round marbles, all colours."

"Yes. You have no soul, Lomas."

"I dare say. I'm busy."

"With toxic spouses!" said Reggie reproachfully. "Green, was it? Green quartz, I suppose, or perhaps jade with the pattern in oxide of iron."

"And I expect some child has swopped it for a green apple."

"Lomas dear," Mr. Fortune expostulated, "this is romance. Ten thousand years ago the cave men in France painted these patterns on stones. And still in Borneo there's men making them for magic. Big magic. A charm against death. And some bright lad comes down to Bloomsbury and throws a fit to steal one. My hat, he's the heir of all the ages! I could bear to meet this epilept."

"I couldn't," said Lomas. "I have to meet quite enough of the weak-minded officially."

But Reggie Fortune was deaf to satire. "A magic stone," he murmured happily.

"Oh, take the case by all means," said Lomas. "I'm glad I've brought you something that really interests you. Let me know when you find the pebble," and announcing that he had a day's work to do on the morrow, he went with an air of injury to bed.

It was an enemy (a K.C. after a long and vain cross-examination) who said that Mr. Fortune has a larger mass of useless knowledge than any man in England. Mr. Fortune has been heard to explain his eminence in the application of science to crime by explaining that he knows nothing thoroughly but a little of everything, thus preserving an open mind. This may account for his instant conviction that there was something for him in the matter of the magic stone. Or will you prefer to believe with Superintendent Bell that he has some singular faculty for feeling other men's minds at work, a sort of sixth sense? This is mystical, and no one is less of a mystic than Reggie Fortune.

To the extreme discomfort of Lomas he filled the time which their car took in reaching London with a lecture on the case. He found that three explanations were possible. The stone might have been stolen by some one who believed in its magical power, or by some one who coveted it for a collection, or by some one who meant to sell it to a collector.

"Why stop?" Lomas yawned. "It might have been snapped up by a kleptomaniac or an ostrich or a lunatic. Or perhaps some chap wanted to crack a nut. Or a winkle. Does one crack winkles?"

Reggie went on seriously. He thought it unlikely that the thing was stolen as a charm.

"Oh, don't lose heart," said Lomas. "Why not put it down to a brave from Borneo? The original owner comes over in his war paint to claim his long lost magic stone. Malay runs amuck in Museum. That would go well in the papers. Very plausible too. Compare the mysterious Indians who are always hunting down their temple jewels in novels."

"Lomas, you have a futile mind. Of course some fellow might want it for an amulet. It's not only savages who believe in charms. How many men carried a mascot through the war? But your epileptic friend with the New York address don't suggest this simple faith. I suspect a collector."

"Well, I'll believe anything of collectors," Lomas admitted. "They collect heads in Borneo, don't they? I know a fellow who collects shoes. Scalps or stamps or press-cuttings, it's all very sad."

"I want you to cable to New York and verify this epilept. Which I do not think. I'm going to look about for him here."

"My dear Fortune!" Lomas sat up and put up an eyeglass to examine him. "Are you well? This is zeal. But what exactly are you looking for?"

"That's what I want to find out," said Reggie, and having left Lomas at Scotland Yard made a round of calls.

It is believed that there is no class or trade, from bargees to bishops, in which Reggie Fortune has not friends. The first he sought was a dealer in exotic curiosities. From him, not without diplomatic suppression of the truth, Mr. Fortune made sure that magic stones from Borneo were nothing accounted of in the trade, seldom seen and never sought. It was obvious that the subject did not interest his dealer, who could not tell where Mr. Fortune would find such a thing. Old Demetrius Jacob was as likely a man as any.

"Queer name," said Mr. Fortune.

"Queer fish," he was informed. "Syrian, you know, with a bit of Greek. A lot of odd small stuff goes his way."

Mr. Fortune filed Demetrius Jacob for reference and visited another friend, a wholesale draper, whose real interest in life was his collection of objects of savage art. A still more diplomatic economy of the truth brought out the fact that the draper did not possess a magic stone of Borneo, and would do and pay a good deal to obtain one. He was excited by the mere thought. And Reggie Fortune watching him as he expanded on the theme of magic stones, said to himself: "Yes, old thing, a collector is the nigger in this wood pile." The draper returning to the cold reality mourned that his collection lacked this treasure, and cheered up again at the thought that nobody else had it.

"Nobody?" said Reggie Fortune. "Really?"

The draper was annoyed. "Well, I know old Tetherdown hasn't. And he has the best collection in England. Of course with his money he can do anything."

Reggie Fortune neatly diverting the conversation to harmless subjects, consulted his encyclopædic memory about old Tetherdown.

Lord Tetherdown was a little gentleman of middle age, reputed by connoisseurs to be the shabbiest in London. He inherited great wealth and used it by living like a hermit and amassing an anthropological collection. That afternoon saw Reggie Fortune knocking at a little house in a back street of Mayfair. The door was opened by an old woman in an overall. Lord Tetherdown was not at home. Reggie Fortune exhibited great surprise. "Really? But I counted on seeing him. Can you tell me when he'll be back?"

"No, I can't; he's away."

It appeared to Reggie that she was ill at ease. "Away?" he repeated. "Oh, that's absurd. When did he go?"

"He was off last night."

"Really? But didn't he say when he'd be back?"

"No, he didn't, young man."

"It's amazing."

"I don't know what call you have to be amazed, neither," she cried.

"But I counted on seeing him to-day," Reggie explained. "I had better come in and write a note."

The old woman did not seem to think so, but she let him in and took him to a little room. Reggie Fortune caught his breath. For the place was ineffably musty. It was also very full. There was hardly space for both him and the woman. Cabinets lined the walls; and in the corners, in between the cabinets, on top, on the mantel and the window sill were multitudes of queer things. A large and diabolical mask of red feathers towered above him, and he turned from it to see a row of glittering little skulls made of rock crystal and lapis lazuli and carved with hideous realism. On the door hung a cloak made of many coloured bird skins and a necklace of human teeth with the green image of a demon as pendant. A golden dragon with crystal eyes gaped on the sideboard over the whisky decanter.

Reggie showed no surprise. He slid into a chair by the table and looked at the old woman. "I don't know what you want that you can't say," she grumbled, unlocked a desk and put before him one sheet of paper, one envelope, pen and ink.

"Well, it's about a curio," Reggie smiled upon her.

"The good Lord knows we've enough of them," she cried. "That's what took him away now."

Reggie showed no interest and naturally, while he went on writing that Mr. Fortune was anxious to consult Lord Tetherdown on a matter of anthropology, she went on talking. He learnt that it was a gentleman coming about a curio who took Lord Tetherdown away the night before, and she made it plain that she thought little of gentlemen who came about curios.

"Didn't he say when he would be back?" Reggie asked as he stood up to go.

"Not a word, I tell you."

"Well, that's strange."

"Strange, is it? It's plain you don't know the master, young man. He'd go to the end of kingdom come for his pretties."

"I hope he hasn't gone as far as that," said Reggie. He saw as he turned the corner of the street that she was still looking after him. "She knows more than she says," he told himself, "or she's more rattled than she'll let on." He went to Scotland Yard.

Lomas was pleased to see him. "And how do you like marbles, Fortune?" he said genially. "An intellectual game, I'm told. The glass ones are the trumps now, Bell says. I'm afraid you're old-fashioned. Stone isn't used by the best people."

"Breakin' upon this merry persiflage," said Reggie, "have you heard from New York?"

"New York is silent. Probably stunned by your searching question. But the American Embassy speaks. Where's that report, Bell?"

Superintendent Bell, with an apologetic smile, for he always liked Mr. Fortune, read out: "James L. Beeton is a well-known and opulent citizen now travelling in Europe for his health. Present address not known."

"For his health, mark you," Lomas added.

"Yes. There is some good intelligence work in this business. But not at Scotland Yard."

"He is very harsh with us, Bell. I fear he has had a bad day. The marbles ran badly for him. My dear Fortune, I always told you there was nothing in it."

"You did," said Reggie grimly. "I'll forgive you, but I won't promise to forget. Do you know Lord Tetherdown?"

"The little rag bag who collects rags and bones? He has been a joke this ten years."

"Lord Tetherdown is a very wealthy man," said Superintendent Bell with respect.

"Yes. He's gone. Now Lomas, stemming your cheery wit, apply your mind to this. Yesterday morning a rare specimen was stolen from the British Museum. Yesterday evening Lord Tetherdown, who collects such things, who hasn't got that particular thing and would pay through the nose to get it, was called on by a man about a curio. Lord Tetherdown went out and vanished."

"My dear fellow!" Lomas put up his eyeglass. "I admire your imagination. But what is it you want me to believe? That Tetherdown arranged for this accursed stone to be stolen?"

"I doubt that," said Reggie thoughtfully.

"So do I. He's a meek shy little man. Well then, did the thief try to sell it to Tetherdown? Why should that make Tetherdown run away?"

"It might decoy him away."

Lomas stared at him, apparently trying to believe that he was real. "My dear fellow!" he protested. "Oh, my dear fellow! This is fantastic. Why should anyone suddenly decoy little Tetherdown? He never made an enemy. He would have nothing on him to steal. It's an old joke that he don't carry the worth of a shilling. He has lived in that hovel with his two old fogeys of servants for years and sometimes he goes off mysteriously and the fellows in his club only notice he has been away when he blows in again."

"You're a born policeman, Lomas," Reggie sighed. "You're so commonplace."

"Quite, quite," said Lomas heartily. "Now tell me. You've been to Tetherdown's place. Did his servants say they were surprised he had gone off?"

"The old dame said he often went off on a sudden," Reggie admitted, and Lomas laughed. "Well, what about it? You won't do anything?"

"My dear Fortune, I'm only a policeman, as you say. I can't act without some reason."

"Oh, my aunt!" said Reggie. "Reasons! Good night. Sleep sound."

In comfortable moments since he has been heard to confess that Lomas was perfectly right, that there was nothing which the police could have done, but he is apt to diverge into an argument that policemen are creatures whose function in the world is to shut the stable door after the horse is stolen. A pet theory of his.

He went to the most solemn of his clubs and having soothed his feelings with muffins, turned up Lord Tetherdown in the peerage. The house of Tetherdown took little space. John William Bishop Coppett was the seventh baron, but his ancestors were not distinguished and the family was dwindling. John William Lord Tetherdown had no male kin alive but his heir, who was his half-brother, the Hon. George Bishop Coppett. The Hon. George seemed from his clubs to be a sportsman. Mr. Fortune meditated.

On his way home he called upon the Hon. George, whose taste in dwellings and servants was different from his half-brother's. Mr. Coppett had a flat in a vast, new and gorgeous block. His door was opened by a young man who used a good tailor and was very wide awake. But Mr. Coppett, like Lord Tetherdown, was not at home. His man, looking more knowing than ever, did not think it would be of any use to call again. Oh, no, sir, Mr. Coppett was not out of town: he would certainly be back that night: but (something like a wink flickered on the young man's face) too late to see anyone. If the gentleman would ring up in the morning-not too early-Reggie Fortune said that it didn't much matter.

He went off to dine with her whom he describes as his friskier sister: the one who married a bishop. It made him sleep sound.

Thus the case of the magic stone was left to ferment for some fifteen hours. For which Mr. Fortune has been heard to blame himself and the conjugal bliss of bishops.

Over a devilled sole at breakfast-nature demanded piquant food-his mind again became active. He rang for his car. Sam, his admirable chauffeur, was told that he preferred to drive himself, which is always in him a sign of mental excitement. "Country work, sir?" Sam asked anxiously, for he holds that only on Salisbury Plain should Mr. Fortune be allowed to drive. Mr. Fortune shook his head, and Sam swallowed and they came down upon Oxford Street like the wolf on the fold. The big car was inserted, a camel into the eye of a needle, into the alleyway where Lord Tetherdown's house lurks.

Again the old woman in the overall was brought to the door. She recognized Reggie Fortune and liked him less than ever. "There's no answer," she cried. "The master's not back."

"Really?"

"You heard what I said."

"He's not let you know when he's coming back?"

"No, he hasn't, nor I've no call to tell you if he had. You and your curios!" The door slammed.

Reggie went back to his car. When it stopped again in a shabby street by Covent Garden, Sam allowed himself to cough, his one protest from first to last: a devoted fellow. Reggie Fortune surveyed the shop of Demetrius Jacob, which displayed in its dirty window shelves sparsely covered with bad imitations of old pewter. Reggie frowned at it, looked at the name again and went in. The place was like a lumber room. He saw nothing but damaged furniture which had never been good and little of that until he found out that the dusty thing on which he was standing was an exquisite Chinese carpet. Nobody was in the shop, nobody came, though the opening door had rung a bell. He made it ring again and still had to wait. Then there swept through the place a woman, a big woman and handsome in her dark oriental way. She did not see Reggie, she was too hurried or too angry, if her flush and her frown were anger. She banged the door and was gone.

Reggie rapped on a rickety desk. After a moment an old man shuffled into the shop, made something like a salaam and said: "You want, Yes?" Not so old after all, Reggie decided on a second glance. He shuffled because his slippers were falling off, he was bent because he cringed, his yellow face was keen and healthy and his eyes bright under black brows, but certainly a queer figure in that tight frock coat which came nearly to his heels, and his stiff green skull cap.

"Mr. Jacob?" Reggie said.

"I am Demetrius Jacob," he pronounced it in the Greek way.

"Well, I am interested in savage religions and cults you know, and I'm told you are the man for me." Mr. Jacob again made salaam. "What I'm after just now is charms and amulets." He paused and suddenly rapped out: "Have you got anything from Borneo?"

Demetrius Jacob showed no surprise or any other emotion. "Borneo? Oh, yes, I t'ink," he smiled. "Beautiful t'ings." He shuffled to a cupboard and brought out a tray which contained two skulls and a necklace of human teeth.

Reggie Fortune was supercilious. He demanded amulets, stone amulets and in particular a stone amulet like a cigar with zigzag painting.

Demetrius Jacob shook his head. "I not 'ave 'im," he said sadly. "Not from Borneo. I 'ave beautiful *galets colorés* from France, yes, and Russia. But not the east. I never see 'im from the east but in the Museum."

Reggie Fortune went away thinking that it took a clever fellow to be as guileless as that.

The car plunged through Piccadilly again to the flat of the Hon. George Coppett. Mr. Coppett's man received him with a smile which was almost a leer. "I'll see, sir," he took Reggie's card. "I'm afraid Mr. Coppett's partic'larly busy." As Reggie was ushered in he heard a bell ring and a woman's voice high and angry, "Oh, yes, I will go. But I do not believe you, not one word." A door was flung open and across the hall swept the big woman of Demetrius Jacob's shop. Reggie looked into the crown of his hat. She stopped short and stared hard at him. Either she did not recognize him or did not care who he was. She hurried on and the door banged behind her.

The Hon. George Coppett was a little man who walked like a bird. "Damn it, damn it," he piped, jumping about, "what the devil are you at, Brown?" He stared at Mr. Fortune, and Brown gave him Mr. Fortune's card. "Hallo, don't know you, do I? I'm in the devil of a hurry."

"I think you had better see me, Mr. Coppett," said Reggie. Mr. Coppett swore again and bade him come in.

Mr. Coppett gave himself some whisky. "I say, women are the devil," he said as he wiped his mouth. "Have one?" he nodded to the decanter. "No? Well, what's your trouble, Mr. — Mr. Fortune?"

"I am anxious to have some news of Lord Tetherdown."

"Well, why don't you ask him?" Mr. Coppett laughed.

"He's not to be found."

"What, gone off again, has he? Lord, he's always at it. My dear chap, he's simply potty about his curios. I don't know the first thing about them, but it beats me how a fellow can fall for that old junk. One of the best and all that don't you know, but it's a mania with him. He's always running off after some queer bit of tripe."

"When do you expect him back?"

"Search me," Mr. Coppett laughed. "My dear chap, he don't tell me his little game. Old Martha might know."

"She doesn't."

Mr. Coppett laughed again. "He always was a close old thing. He just pushes off, don't you know, on any old scent. And after a bit he blows in again."

"Then-you don't know-when you'll see him again?" Reggie said slowly.

"Give you my word I don't," Mr. Coppett cried. "Sorry, sorry."

"So am I," said Reggie. "Good morning, Mr. Coppett."

Mr. Coppett did not try to keep him. But he was hardly beyond the outer door of the flat when he heard Mr. Coppett say, "Hallo, hallo!" He turned. The door was still shut. Mr. Coppett was using the telephone. He heard "Millfield, double three" something and could not hear anything more. Millfield, as you know, is a quiet middle-class suburb. Mr. Fortune went down stairs pensively.

Pensive he was still when he entered Scotland Yard and sought Lomas's room. "Well, how goes the quest for the holy stone?" Lomas put up his eyeglass. "My dear Fortune, you're the knight of the rueful countenance."

"You're confused, Lomas. Don't do it," Reggie complained. "You're not subtle at Scotland Yard, but hang it, you might be clear."

"What can we do for you?"

"One of your largest cigars," Reggie mumbled and took it. "Yes. What can you do? I wonder." He looked at Lomas with a baleful eye. "Who lives at Millfield? Speaking more precisely who lives at Millfield double three something?" Lomas suggested that it was a large order. "It is," Reggie agreed gloomily, "it's a nasty large order." And he described his morning's work. "There you are. The further you go the queerer."

"Quite, quite," Lomas nodded. "But what's your theory, Fortune?"

"The workin' hypothesis is that there's dirty work doin' when a magic stone gets stolen and the man who wants the magic stone vanishes on the same day: which is confirmed when a female connected with a chap who knows all about magic stones is found colloguin' with the vanished man's heir: and further supported when that heir being rattled runs to telephone to the chaste shades of Millfield-the last place for a sporting blood like him to keep his pals. I ask you, who lives at Millfield double three something?"

Lomas shifted his papers. "George Coppett stands to gain by Tetherdown's death, of course," he said. "And the only man so far as we know. But he's not badly off, he's well known, there's never been anything against him. Why should he suddenly plan to do away with his brother? All your story might be explained in a dozen ways. There's not an ounce of evidence, Fortune."

"You like your evidence after the murder. I know that. My God, Lomas, I'm afraid."

"My dear fellow!" Lomas was startled. "This isn't like you."

"Oh, many thanks. I don't like men dying, that's all. Professional prejudice. I'm a doctor, you see. What the devil are we talking for? Who lives at Millfield double three something?"

"We might get at it," Lomas said doubtfully and rang for Superintendent Bell. "But it's a needle in a bundle of hay. And if Tetherdown was to be murdered, it's done by now."

"Yes, that's comforting," said Mr. Fortune.

Superintendent Bell brought a list of the subscribers to the Millfield exchange and they looked over the names of those in the thirty-fourth hundred. Most were shopkeepers and ruled out. "George Coppett don't buy his fish in Millfield," said Reggie Fortune. Over the doctors he hesitated.

"You think it's some fellow in your own trade?" Lomas smiled. "Well, there's nothing like leather."

"Brownrigg," Reggie Fortune muttered. "I know him. 3358 Dr. Jerdan, The Ferns, Chatham Park Road. Where's a medical directory? 3358 Dr. Jerdan is not in the medical directory. Ring up the divisional inspector and ask him what he knows about Dr. Jerdan."

There was nothing, Superintendent Bell announced, known against Dr. Jerdan. He had been at the Ferns some time. He didn't practise. He was said to take in private patients.

"Come on," said Reggie Fortune, and took the Superintendent's arm.

"My dear Fortune," Lomas protested. "This is a bow at a venture. We can't act, you know. Bell can't appear."

"Bell's coming to be a policeman and appear when it's all over. I'm going in to Dr. Jerdan who isn't on the register. And I don't like it, Lomas. Bell shall stay outside. And if I don't come out again-well, then you'll have evidence, Lomas."

Neither Reggie Fortune nor his chauffeur knew the way about in Millfield. They sat together and Mr. Fortune with a map of London exhorted Sam at the wheel and behind them Superintendent Bell held tight and thought of his sins.

The car came by many streets of little drab houses to a road in which the houses were large and detached, houses which had been rural villas when Victoria was queen. "Now go easy," Reggie Fortune said. "Chatham Park Road, Bell. Quiet and respectable as the silent tomb. My God, look at that! Stop, Sam."

What startled him was a hospital nurse on a doorstep.

"Who is she, sir?" Bell asked.

"She's Demetrius Jacob's friend and George Coppett's friend-and now she's Dr. Jerdan's friend and in nurse's rig. Keep the car back here. Don't frighten them."

He jumped out and hurried on to the Ferns. "I don't like it, young fellow, and that's a fact," said Bell, and Sam nodded.

The woman had been let in. Mr. Fortune stood a moment surveying the house which was as closely curtained as all the rest and like them stood back with a curving drive to the door. He rang the bell, had no answer, rang again, knocked and knocked more loudly. It sounded thunderous in the heavy quiet of the Chatham Park Road.

At last the door was opened by a man, a lanky powerful fellow who scowled at Mr. Fortune and said, "We ain't deaf."

"I have been kept waiting," said Reggie. "Dr. Jerdan, please."

"Not at home."

"Oh, I think so. Dr. Jerdan will see me."

"Don't see anyone but by appointment."

"Dr. Jerdan will see me. Go and tell him so." The door was shut in his face. After a moment or two he began knocking again. It was made plain to all the Chatham Park Road that something was happening at the Ferns and here and there a curtain fluttered.

Superintendent Bell got out of the car. "You stay here, son," he said. "Don't stop the engine."

But before he reached the house, the door was opened and Reggie Fortune saw a sleek man who smiled with all his teeth. "So sorry you have been waiting," he purred. "I am Dr. Jerdan's secretary. What can I do for you?"

"Dr. Jerdan will see me."

"Oh, no, I'm afraid not. Dr. Jerdan's not at home."

"Why say so?" said Reggie wearily. "Dr. Jerdan, please."

"You had better tell me your business, sir."

"Haven't you guessed? Lord Tetherdown."

"Lord who?" said the sleek man without a check. "I don't know anything about Lord Tetherdown."

"But then you're only Dr. Jerdan's secretary," Reggie murmured.

Something of respect was to be seen in the pale eyes that studied him, and, after a long stare, "I'll see what I can do. Come in, sir. What's your name?" He thrust his head forward like an animal snapping, but still he smiled.

"Fortune. Reginald Fortune."

"This way." The sleek man led him down a bare hall and showed him into a room at the back. "Do sit down, Mr. Fortune. But I'm afraid you won't see Dr. Jerdan." He slid out. Reggie heard the key turn in the lock. He glanced at the window. That was barred.

"Quite so," said Reggie. "Now how long will Bell wait?"

He took his stand so that he would be behind the door if it were opened, and listened. There was a scurry of feet and some other sound. The feet fell silent, the other sound became a steady tapping. "Good God, are they nailing him down?" he muttered, took up a chair and dashed it at the lock again and again. As he broke out he heard the beat of a motor engine.

Superintendent Bell drawing near saw a car with two men up come out of the coach-house of the Ferns. He ran into the road and stood in its way. It drove straight at him, gathering speed. He made a jump for the footboard, and being a heavy man missed. The car shot by.

The respectability of Chatham Park Road then heard such a stream of swearing as never had flowed that way. For Sam has a mother's love of his best car. But he was heroic. He swung its long body out across the road, swearing, but nevertheless. The fugitives from the Ferns took a chance which was no chance. Their car mounted the pavement, hit a gate-post and crashed.

Superintendent Bell arrived to find Sam backing his own car to the kerb while he looked complacently at its shining sides. "Not a scratch, praise God," he said.

Superintendent Bell pulled up. "You're a wonder, you are," he said, and gazed at the ruins. The smashed car was on its side in a jumble of twisted iron and bricks. The driver was underneath. They could not move him. There were reasons why that did not matter to him. "He's got his," said Sam. "Where's the other? There were two of them."

The other lay half hidden in a laurel hedge. He bad been flung out, he had broken the railings with his head, he had broken the stone below, but his head was a gruesome shape.

In the hall of the Ferns Reggie Fortune stood still to listen. That muffled tapping was the only sound in the house. It came from below. He went down dark stairs into the kitchen. No one was there. The sound came from behind a doorway in the corner. He flung it open and looked down into the blackness of a cellar. He struck a light and saw a bundle lying on the ground, a bundle from which stuck out two feet that tapped at the cellar steps. He brought it up to the kitchen. It was a woman with her head and body in a sack. When he had cut her loose he saw the dark face of the woman of the shop and the flat. She sprang at him and grasped his arms.

"Who are you?" she cried. "Where is Lord Tetherdown?"

"My name is Fortune, madame. And yours?"

"I am Melitta Jacob. What is that to you? Where have you put Lord Tetherdown?"

"I am looking for him."

"You! Is he not here? Oh, you shall pay for it, you and those others."

But Reggie was already running upstairs. One room and another he tried in vain and at last at the top of the house found a locked door. The key was in the lock. Inside on a pallet bed, but clothed, lay a little man with some days' beard. The woman thrust Reggie away and flung herself down by the bedside and gathered the man to her bosom moaning over him. "My lord, my lord."

"Oh, my aunt!" said Reggie Fortune. "Now, Miss Jacob, please," he put his hand on her shoulder.

"He is mine," she said fiercely.

"Well, just now he's mine. I'm a doctor."

"Oh, is he not dead?" she cried.

"Not exactly," said Reggie Fortune. "Not yet." He took the body from quivering arms.

"What is it, then?"

"He is drugged, and I should say starved. If you——" a heavy footstep drew near. She sprang up ready for battle, and in the doorway fell upon Superintendent Bell.

"Easy, easy," he received her on his large chest and made sure of her wrists. "Mr. Fortune-just got in by the window-what about this?"

"That's all right," Reggie mumbled from the bed. "Send me Sam."

"Coming, sir." Sam ran in. "Those fellows didn't do a getaway. They're outed. Car smash. Both killed. Some smash."

"Brandy, meat juice, ammonia," murmured Mr. Fortune, who was writing, "and that. Hurry."

"Beg pardon, ma'am," Bell detached himself from Melitta Jacob. He took off his hat and tiptoed to the bed. "Have they done for him, sir," he muttered.

Mr. Fortune was again busy over the senseless body. One of its hands was clenched. He opened the fingers gently, and drew out a greenish lump painted with a zigzag pattern in red. "The magic stone," he said. "A charm against death. Well, well."

* * * * * *

On his lawn which slopes to the weir stream Reggie Fortune lay in a deck chair, and a syringa, waxen white, shed its fragrance about him. He opened his eyes to see the jaunty form of the Hon. Sidney Lomas tripping towards him. "Stout fellow," he murmured. "That's cider cup. There was ice in it once," and he shut his eyes again.

"I infer that the patient is out of your hands."

"They're going for their honeymoon to Nigeria."

"Good Gad," said Lomas.

"Collecting, you see. The objects of art of the noble savage. She's rather a dear."

"I should have thought he'd done enough collecting. Does he understand yet what happened?"

"Oh, he's quite lucid. Seems to think it's all very natural."

"Does he though?"

"Only he's rather annoyed with brother George. He thinks brother George had no right to object to his marrying. That's what started it, you see. Brother George came round to borrow his usual hundred or so and found him with the magnificent Melitta. It occurred to brother George that if Tetherdown was going to marry, something had to be done about it. And then I suppose brother George consulted the late Jerdan." Mr. Fortune opened his eyes, and raised himself. "By the way, who was Jerdan? I saw you hushed up the inquest as a motor smash."

"Bell thinks he was the doctor who bolted out of the Antony case."

"Oh, ah. Yes, there was some brains in that. I rather thought the late Jerdan had experience. I wonder what happened to his private patients at the Ferns. Creepy house. I say, was it Jerdan or his man who threw the fit at the Museum?"

"Jerdan himself, by the description."

"Yes. Useful thing, medical training. Well, Jerdan saw he could get at Tetherdown through his hobby. He came with tales of anthropological treasures for sale. The old boy didn't bite at first. Jerdan couldn't hit on anything he wanted. But he found out at last what he did want. Hence the fit in the Museum. That night Jerdan turned up with the Borneo stone and told Tetherdown a friend of his had some more of the kind. Tetherdown fell for that. He went off to the Ferns with Jerdan. The last thing he remembers is sitting down in the back room to look at the stone. They chloroformed him, I think, there was lots of stuff in the place. Then they kept him under morphia and starved him. I suppose the notion was to dump his dead body somewhere so that the fact of his death could be established and George inherit. There could be no clear evidence of murder. Tetherdown is eccentric. It would look as if he had gone off his head and wandered about till he died of exhaustion. That was the late Jerdan's idea. Melitta always thought George was a bad egg. He didn't like her, you see, and he showed it. When Tetherdown vanished she went off to George one time. He laughed at her, which was his error. She put on that nurse's rig for a disguise and watched his rooms. When I rattled him and he rang up Jerdan, Jerdan came to the flat and she followed him back to the Ferns and asked for Tetherdown. Jolly awkward for Jerdan with me knocking at the door. He was crude with her, but I don't know that I blame him. An able fellow. Pity, pity. Yes. What happened to brother George?"

"Bolted. We haven't a trace of him. Which is just as well, for there's no evidence. Jerdan left no papers. George could have laughed at us if he had the nerve."

Reggie Fortune chuckled. "I never liked George. I rang him up that night: 'Mr. George Coppett? The Ferns speaking. It's all out' and I rang off. I thought George would quit. George will be worrying quite a lot. So that's that."

"Yes, you have your uses, Fortune," said Lomas. "I've noticed it before."

Reggie Fortune fumbled in his pocket and drew out the magic stone. "Tetherdown said he would like me to have it. Cut him to the heart to give it up, poor old boy. Told me it saved his life." He smiled. "I don't care for its methods, myself. Better put it back in a glass case, Lomas."

"What did Melitta give you?"

"Melitta is rather a dear," said Mr. Fortune.

CASE V

THE SNOWBALL BURGLARY

A TELEGRAM was brought to Mr. Fortune. It announced that the woman whom his ingenuity convicted of the Winstanton murder had confessed it in prison just after the Home Secretary decided not to hang her. Mr. Fortune sighed satisfaction and took his hostess in to dinner.

He was staying in a Devonshire country house for mental repairs. This is not much like him, for save on visits of duty country houses seldom receive him. The conversation of the county, he complains, is too great a strain upon his intellect. Also, he has no interest in killing creatures, except professionally. But the output of crime had been large that winter and the task of keeping Scotland Yard straight, laborious; and he sought relief with Colonel Beach at Cranston Regis. For Tom Beach, once in the first flight of hunting men, having married a young wife, put central heat and electric light into a remote Tudor manor house, and retired there to grow iris and poultry. Neither poultry nor young wives allured Reggie Fortune, but gardens he loves, and his own iris were not satisfying him.

So he sat by Alice Beach at her table, and while her talk flowed on like the brook in the poem, while he wondered why men marry, since their bachelor dinners are better eating, surveyed with mild eyes her and her guests. Tom Beach had probably been unable to help marrying her, she was so pink and white and round, her eyes so shy and innocent. She was one of those women who make it instantly clear to men that they exist to be married, and Tom Beach has always done his duty. "But she's not such a fool as she looks," Reggie had pronounced.

With pity if not sympathy he glanced down the table at Tom Beach, that large, red, honest man who sat doing his best between dignity and impudence, dignity in the awful person of Mrs. Faulks and the mighty pretty impudence of his wife's sister, Sally Winslow. Mrs. Faulks has been described as one who could never be caught bending, or a model of the art of the corset. She is spare, she is straight; and few have seen her exhibit interest in anything but other people's incomes, which she always distrusts. A correct woman, but for a habit of wearing too many jewels.

What she was doing in Tom Beach's genial house was plain enough. Her son had brought her to inspect Sally Winslow, as a man brings a vet to the horse he fancies. But it was not plain why Alexander Faulks fancied Sally Winslow. Imagine a bulldog after a butterfly. But bulldogs have a sense of humour. Sally Winslow is a wisp of a creature who has no respect for anyone, even herself. Under her bright bobbed hair, indeed, is the daintiest colour; but when some fellow said she had the face of a fairy, a woman suggested the face of a fairy's maid. She listened to Alexander's heavy talk and watched him in a fearful fascination, but sometimes she shot a glance across the table where a little man with a curly head and a roguish eye was eating his dinner demurely. His worst enemies never said that Captain Bunny Cosdon's manners were bad.

Now you know them all. When they made up a four for bridge, upon which Mrs. Faulks always insists, it was inevitable that Reggie Fortune should stand out, for his simple mind declines to grasp the principles of cards. Alexander Faulks in his masterful way directed Sally to the table; and scared, but submissive, she sat down and giggled nervously. Reggie found himself left to his hostess and Captain Cosdon. They seemed determined to entertain him and he sighed and listened.

So he says. He is emphatic that he did not go to sleep. But the study of the events of that evening which afterwards became necessary, makes it clear that a long time passed before Alice Beach was saying the first thing that he remembers. "Did you ever know a perfect crime, Mr. Fortune?"

Mr. Fortune then sat up, as he records, and took notice.

Captain Cosdon burst out laughing, and departed, humming a stave of "Meet me to-night in Dreamland."

Mr. Fortune gazed at his hostess. He had not supposed that she could say anything so sensible. "Most crimes are perfect," he said.

"But how horrible! I should hate to be murdered and know there wasn't a clue who did it."

"Oh, there'll be a clue all right," Reggie assured her.

"Are you sure? And will you promise to catch my murderer, Mr. Fortune?"

"Well, you know," he considered her round amiable face, "if you were murdered it would be a case of art for art's sake. That's very rare. I was speakin' scientifically. A perfect crime is a complete series of cause and effect. Where you have that, there's always a clue, there is always evidence, and when you get to work on it the unknown quantities come out. Yes. Most crimes are perfect. But you must allow for chance. Sometimes the criminal is an idiot. That's a nuisance. Sometimes he has a streak of luck and the crime is damaged before we find it, something has been washed out, a bit of it has been lost. It's the imperfect crimes that give trouble."

"But how fascinating!"

"Oh, Lord, no," said Mr. Fortune.

The bridge-players were getting up. Sally Winslow was announcing that she had lost all but honour. Mrs. Faulks wore a ruthless smile. Sally went off to bed.

"Oh, Mrs. Faulks," her sister cried, "do come! Mr. Fortune is lecturing on crime."

"Really. How very interesting," said Mrs. Faulks, and transfixed Reggie with an icy stare.

"The perfect criminal in one lesson," Alice Beach laughed. "I feel a frightful character already. All you want is luck, you know. Or else Mr. Fortune catches you every time."

"I say, you know, Alice," her husband protested.

A scream rang out. Alice stopped laughing. The little company looked at each other. "Where was that?" Tom Beach muttered.

"Not in the house, Colonel," Faulks said. "Certainly not in the house."

Tom Beach was making for the window when all the lights went out.

Alice gave a cry. The shrill voice of Mrs. Faulks arose to say, "Really!" Colonel Beach could be heard swearing. "Don't let us get excited," said Faulks. Reggie Fortune struck a match.

"Excited be damned," said Tom Beach, and rang the bell.

Reggie Fortune, holding his match aloft, made for the door and opened it. The hall was dark, too.

"Oh, Lord, it's the main fuse blown out!" Tom Beach groaned.

"Or something has happened in your little power station," said Reggie Fortune cheerfully, and his host snorted. For the electricity at Cranston Regis comes from turbines on the stream which used to fill the Tudor fish-ponds, and Colonel Beach loves his machinery like a mother.

He shouted to the butler to bring candles, and out of the dark the voice of the butler was heard apologizing. He roared to the chauffeur, who was his engineer, to put in a new fuse. "It's not the fuse, Colonel," came a startled voice, "there's no juice."

Colonel Beach swore the more. "Run down to the powerhouse, confound you. Where the devil are those candles?"

The butler was very sorry, sir, the butler was coming, sir.

"Really!" said Mrs. Faulks in the dark, for Reggie had grown tired of striking matches. "Most inconvenient." So in the dark they waited...

And again they heard a scream. It was certainly in the house this time, it came from upstairs, it was in the voice of Sally Winslow. Reggie Fortune felt some one bump against him, and knew by the weight it was Faulks. Reggie struck another match, and saw him vanish into the darkness above as he called, "Miss Winslow, Miss Winslow!"

There was the sound of a scuffle and a thud. Colonel Beach stormed upstairs. A placid voice spoke out of the dark at Reggie's ear, "I say, what's up with the jolly old house?" The butler arrived quivering with a candle in each hand and a bodyguard of candle-bearing satellites, and showed him the smiling face of Captain Cosdon.

From above Colonel Beach roared for lights. "The C.O. sounds peeved," said Captain Cosdon. "Someone's for it, what?"

They took the butler's candles and ran up, discovering with the light Mr. Faulks holding his face together. "Hallo, hallo! Dirty work at the crossroads, what? Why — — Sally! Good God!"

On the floor of the passage Sally Winslow lay like a child asleep, one frail bare arm flung up above her head.

"Look at that, Fortune," Tom Beach cried. "Damned scoundrels!"

"Hold the candle," said Reggie Fortune; but as he knelt beside her the electric light came on again.

"Great Jimmy!" Captain Cosdon exclaimed. "Who did that?"

"Don't play the fool, Bunny," Tom Beach growled. "What have they done to her, Fortune?"

Reggie's plump, capable hands were moving upon the girl delicately. "Knocked her out," he said, and stared down at her, and rubbed his chin.

"Who? What? How?" Cosdon cried. "Hallo, Faulks, what's your trouble? Who hit you?"

"How on earth should I know," Faulks mumbled, still feeling his face as he peered at the girl. "When Miss Winslow screamed, I ran up. It was dark, of course. Some men caught hold of me. I struck out and they set on me. I was knocked down. I wish you would look at my eye, Fortune."

Reggie was looking at Sally, whose face had begun to twitch.

"Your eye will be a merry colour to-morrow," Cosdon assured him. "But who hit Sally?"

"It was the fellows who set upon me, I suppose, of course; they were attacking her when I rescued her."

"Stout fellow," said Cosdon. "How many were there?"

"Quite a number. Quite. How can I possibly tell? It was dark. Quite a number."

Sally tried to sneeze and failed, opened her eyes and murmured, "The light, the light." She saw the men about her and began to laugh hysterically.

"Good God, the scoundrels may be in the house still," cried Tom Beach. "Come on, Cosdon."

"I should say so," said Captain Cosdon, but he lingered over Sally. "All right now?" he asked anxiously.

"Oh, Bunny," she choked in her laughter. "Yes, yes, I'm all right. Oh, Mr. Fortune, what is it? Oh, poor Mr. Faulks, what has happened?"

"Just so," said Reggie. He picked her up and walked off with her to her bedroom.

"Oh, you are strong," she said, not coquetting, but in honest surprise, like a child.

Reggie laughed. "There's nothing of you," and he laid her down on her bed. "Well, what about it?"

"I feel all muzzy."

"That'll pass off," said Reggie cheerfully. "Do you know what hit you?"

"No. Isn't it horrid? It was all dark, you know. There's no end of a bruise," she felt behind her ear and made a face.

"I know, I know," Reggie murmured sympathetically. "And how did it all begin?"

"Why, I came up to bed, Mr. Fortune-heavens, there may be a man in here now!" she raised herself.

"Yes, we'd better clear that up," said Reggie, and looked under the bed and opened the wardrobe and thrust into her dresses and turned back to her. "No luck, Miss Winslow."

"Oh, thank goodness," she sank down again. "You see, I came up and put the light on, of course, and there was a man at the window there. Then I screamed."

"The first scream," Reggie murmured.

"And then the lights went out. I ran away and tumbled over that chair and then out into the passage. I kept bumping into things and it was horrid. And then-oh, somebody caught hold of me and I screamed — —"

"The second scream," Reggie murmured.

"I was sort of flung about. There were men there fighting in the dark. Horrid. Hitting all round me, you know. And then-oh, well, I suppose I stopped one, didn't I?"

There was a tap at the door. "May I come in, doctor?" said Alice Beach.

"Oh, Alice, have they caught anyone?"

"Not a creature. Isn't it awful? Oh, Sally, you poor darling," her sister embraced her. "What a shame! Is it bad?"

"I'm all muddled. And jolly sore."

"My dear! It is too bad it should be you. Oh, Mr. Fortune, what did happen?"

"Some fellow knocked her out. She'll be all right in the morning. But keep her quiet and get her off to sleep." He went to the window. It was open and the curtains blowing in the wind. He looked out. A ladder stood against the wall. "And that's that. Yes. Put her to bed, Mrs. Beach."

Outside in the passage he found Captain Cosdon waiting. "I say, Fortune, is she much hurt?"

"She's taken a good hard knock. She's not made for it. But she'll be all right."

"Sally! Oh damn," said Cosdon.

"Did you catch anybody?"

"Napoo. All clear. The Colonel's going round to see if they got away with anything. And Faulks wants you to look at his poor eye."

"Nothing of yours gone?"

Cosdon laughed. "No. But I'm not exactly the burglar's friend, don't you know? My family jewels wouldn't please the haughty crook. I say, it's a queer stunt. Ever been in one like it?"

"I don't think it went according to plan," said Reggie Fortune.

He came down and found Faulks with an eye dwindling behind a bruise of many colours, arguing with an agitated butler that the house must contain arnica. Before he could give the attention which Mr. Faulks imperiously demanded, the parade voice of the Colonel rang through the house. "Fortune, come up here!"

Tom Beach stood in the study where he writes the biographies of his poultry and his iris. There also are kept the cups, medals and other silver with which shows reward their beauty. "Look at that!" he cried, with a tragic gesture. The black pedestals of the cups, the velvet cases of the medals stood empty.

"Great Jimmy!" said Captain Cosdon in awe.

"Well, that's very thorough," said Reggie. "And the next thing, please."

Colonel Beach said it was a damned outrage. He also supposed that the fellows had stripped the whole place. And he bounced out.

Reggie went to his own room. He had nothing which could be stolen but his brushes, and they were not gone. He looked out of the window. In the cold March moonlight he saw two men moving hither and thither, and recognized one for his chauffeur and factotum Sam, and shouted.

"Nothing doing, sir," Sam called back. "Clean getaway."

Reggie went downstairs to the smoking-room. He was stretched in a chair consuming soda-water and a large cigar when there broke upon him in a wave of chattering Tom Beach and Alice and Captain Cosdon.

"Oh, Mr. Fortune, is this a perfect crime?" Alice laughed.

Reggie shook his head. "I'm afraid it had an accident in its youth. The crime that took the wrong turning."

"How do you mean, Fortune?" Tom Beach frowned. "It's deuced awkward."

"Awkward is the word," Reggie agreed. "What's gone, Colonel?"

"Well, there's my pots, you know. And Alice has lost a set of cameos she had in her dressing-room."

"Pigs!" said Alice with conviction.

"And Mrs. Faulks says they've taken that big ruby brooch she was wearing before dinner. You know it."

"It's one of the things I could bear not to know," Reggie murmured. "Nothing else?"

"She says she doesn't know, she's too upset to be sure. I say, Fortune, this is a jolly business for me."

"My dear chap!"

"She's gone to bed fuming. Faulks is in a sweet state too."

"What's he lost?"

"Only his eye," Cosdon chuckled.

"That's the lot, then? Nice little bag, but rather on the small side. Yes, it didn't go according to plan."

"Oh, Mr. Fortune, what are you going to do?"

"Do?" said Reggie reproachfully. "I? Where's the nearest policeman?"

"Why, here," Alice pointed at him.

"Cranston Abbas," said Tom Beach, "and he's only a yokel. Village constable, don't you know."

"Yes, you are rather remote, Colonel. What is there about you that brings the wily cracksman down here?"

"Mrs. Faulks!" Alice cried. "That woman must travel with a jeweller's shop. There's a chance for you, Mr. Fortune. Get her rubies back and you'll win her heart."

"Jewelled in fifteen holes. I'd be afraid of burglars. Mrs. Beach, you're frivolous, and the Colonel's going to burst into tears. Will anyone tell me what did happen? We were all in the drawing-room —no. Where were you, Cosdon?"

"Writing letters here, old thing."

"Quite so. And the servants?"

"All in the servants' hall at supper!" Colonel Beach said. "They are all right."

"Quite. Miss Winslow went upstairs and saw a man at her window. There's a ladder at it. She screamed and the lights went out. Why?"

"The rascals got at the powerhouse. Baker found the main switch off."

"Then they knew their way about here. Have you sacked any servant lately? Had any strange workman in the place? No? Yet the intelligence work was very sound. Well, in the darkness Miss Winslow tumbled out into the passage and was grabbed and screamed, and the brave Faulks ran upstairs and took a black eye, and Miss Winslow took the count, and when we arrived there wasn't a burglar in sight. Yes, there was some luck about."

"Not for Sally," said her sister.

"No," said Reggie thoughtfully. "No, but there was a lot of luck going." He surveyed them through his cigar smoke with a bland smile.

"What do you think I ought to do, Fortune?" said Tom Beach.

"Go to bed," said Reggie. "What's the time? Time runs on, doesn't it? Yes, go to bed."

"Oh, but, Mr. Fortune, you are disappointing," Alice Beach cried.

"I am. I notice it every day. It's my only vice."

"I do think you might be interested!"

"A poor crime, but her own," Captain Cosdon chuckled. "It's no good, Mrs. Beach. It don't appeal to the master mind."

"You know, Fortune, it's devilish awkward," the Colonel protested.

"I'm sorry. But what can we do? You might call up your village policeman. He's four miles off, and I dare say he needs exercise. You might telephone to Thorton and say you have been burgled, and will they please watch some road or other for some one or other with a bag of silver and a set of cameos and a ruby brooch. It doesn't sound helpful, does it?"

"It sounds damned silly."

"But I thought you'd find clues, Mr. Fortune," Alice Beach cried, "all sorts of clues, finger-prints and foot-prints and ——"

"And tell us the crime was done by a retired sergeant-cook with pink hair and a cast in the eye," Cosdon grinned.

"You see, I've no imagination," said Reggie, sadly.

"Confound you, Cosdon, it isn't a joke," Colonel Beach cried.

"No, I don't think it's a joke," Reggie agreed.

"One of your perfect crimes, Mr. Fortune?"

"Well, I was sayin' —you have to allow for chance. There was a lot of luck about."

"What are you thinking of?"

"The time, Mrs. Beach. Yes, the flight of time. We'd better go to bed."

But he did not go to bed. He stirred the fire in his bedroom and composed himself by it. The affair annoyed him. He did not want to be bothered by work and his mind insisted on working. Something like this. "Philosophically time is an illusion. 'Time travels in divers paces with divers persons.' Highly divers, yes. Time is the trouble, Colonel. Why was there such a long time between the first scream and the second scream? Sally tumbled down. Sally was fumbling in the dark: but it don't take many minutes to get from her room to the stairs. She took as long as it took the chauffeur to run to the powerhouse. He started some while after the first scream, he had found what was wrong and put the light on again within a minute of the second. Too much time for Sally-and too little. How did Sally's burglars get off so quick? Faulks ran up at the second scream. The rest of us were there next minute. They were there to hit Faulks. When we came, we saw no one, heard no one and found no one." He shook his head at the firelight. "And yet Sally's rather a dear. I wonder. No, it didn't go according to plan. But I don't like it, my child. It don't look pretty."

He sat up. Somebody was moving in the corridor. He went to his table for an electric torch, slid silently across the room, flung open the door and flashed on the light. He caught a glimpse of legs vanishing round a corner, legs which were crawling, a man's legs. A door was closed stealthily.

Reggie swept the light along the floor. It fell at last on some spots of candle grease dropped where the fallen Sally was examined. Thereabouts the legs had been. He moved the light to and fro. Close by stood an old oak settle. He swept the light about it, saw something beneath it flash and picked up Mrs. Faulks's big ruby brooch.

The early morning, which he does not love, found him in the garden. There under Sally's window the ladder still stood. "That came from the potting sheds, sir," his factotum Sam told him. "Matter of a hundred yards." Together they went over the path and away to the little powerhouse by the stream. The ground was still hard from the night frost.

"Not a trace," Reggie murmured. "Well, well. Seen anybody about this morning, Sam?"

"This morning, sir?" Sam stared. "Not a soul."

"Have a look," said Reggie and went in shivering.

He was met by the butler who said nervously that Colonel Beach had been asking for him and would like to see him in the study. There he found not only Colonel Beach but Mrs. Beach and Sally and Captain Cosdon, a distressful company. It was plain that Mrs. Beach had been crying. Sally was on the brink. Cosdon looked like a naughty boy uncertain of his doom. But the Colonel was tragic, the Colonel was taking things very hard.

Reggie Fortune beamed upon them. "Morning, morning. Up already, Miss Winslow? How's the head?"

Sally tried to say something and gulped. Tom Beach broke out: "Sorry to trouble you, Fortune. It's an infernal shame dragging you into this business." He glared at his wife, and she wilted.

"My dear Colonel, it's my job," Reggie protested cheerfully, and edged towards the fire which the Colonel screened.

"I'm awfully sorry, Colonel. I'm the one to blame," Cosdon said. "It's all my fault, don't you know."

"I don't know whose fault it isn't. I know it's a most ghastly mess."

"It's just like a snowball," Alice laughed hysterically. "Our snowball burglary."

"Snowball?" the Colonel roared at her.

"Oh, Tom, you know. When you want subscriptions and have a snowball where every one has to get some one else to subscribe. I thought of it and I brought in Sally and Sally brought in Bunny and then Mr. Faulks came in-poor Mr. Faulks-and then Mrs. Faulks got into it and her rubies."

"And now we're all in it, up to the neck."

"Yes. Yes, that's very lucid," said Reggie. "But a little confusing to an outsider. My brain's rather torpid, you know. I only want to get on the fire." He obtained the central position and sighed happily. "Well now, the workin' hypothesis is that there were no burglars. Somebody thought it would be interesting to put up a perfect crime. For the benefit of the guileless expert."

They were stricken by a new spasm of dismay. They stared at him. "Yes, you always knew it was a fake," Cosdon cried. "I guessed that last night when you kept talking about the time."

"Well, I thought a little anxiety would be good for you. Even the expert has his feelings."

"It was horrid of us, Mr. Fortune," Sally cried. "But it wasn't only meant for you."

"Oh, don't discourage me."

"It was all my fault, Mr. Fortune." Alice put in her claim and looked at him ruefully and then began to laugh. "But you did seem so bored ——"

"Oh, no, no, no. Only my placid nature. Well now, to begin at the beginning. Somebody thought it would be a merry jest to have me on. That was you, Mrs. Beach. For your kindly interest, I thank you."

Mrs. Beach again showed signs of weeping.

"Please don't be horrid, Mr. Fortune," said Sally, fervently.

"I'm trying to be fascinating. But you see I'm so respectable. You unnerve me."

"I thought of a burglary," said Mrs. Beach, choking sobs. "And I asked Sally to do it."

"And she did-all for my sake. Well, one never knows," Reggie sighed, and looked sentimental.

"It wasn't you," said Sally. "I wanted to shock Mr. Faulks."

"Dear, dear. I shouldn't wonder if you have."

"Oh!" Sally shuddered. "That man is on my nerves. He simply follows me about. He scares me. When I found he'd got Tom to ask him here I ——"

"Yes, of course, it's my fault," Tom Beach cried. "I knew it would come round to that."

"You didn't know, dear, how could you?" Sally soothed him. "He doesn't make love to you. Well, he was here and his mamma and-oh, Mr. Fortune, you've seen them. They want shocking. So I talked to Bunny and ——"

"And I came in with both feet," said Captain Cosdon. "My scheme really, Fortune, all my scheme."

"All?" Reggie asked with some emphasis.

"Good Lord, not what's happened."

"I thought we should come to that some day. What did happen?"

And they all began to talk at once. From which tumult emerged the clear little voice of Sally. "Bunny slipped out early and put a garden ladder up at my window and then went off to the powerhouse. When I went to bed, I collected Tom's pots from the study-that was because he is so vain of them-and Alice's cameos-that's because they're so dowdy-and locked them in my trunk. Then I screamed at the window. That was the signal for Bunny and he switched the lights out and came back. All that was what we planned." She looked pathetically at Reggie. "It was a good crime, wasn't it, Mr. Fortune?"

"You have a turn for the profession, Miss Winslow. You will try to be too clever. It's the mark of the criminal mind."

"I say, hang it all, Fortune ——" Cosdon flushed.

"I know I spoilt it," said Sally meekly. "I just stood there, you know, hearing Tom roar downstairs and you all fussing ——"

"And you underrate the policeman. Do I fuss?" Reggie was annoyed.

"You're fussing over my morals now. Well, I stood there and it came over me the burglars just had to have something of Mrs. Faulks's." She gurgled. "That would make it quite perfect. So I ran into her room and struck a match and there was her awful old ruby brooch. I took that and went out into the passage and screamed again. That was the plan. Then I bumped into somebody ——"

"That was me," said Captain Cosdon. "She was such a jolly long time with the second scream I went up to see if anything was wrong— —"

"Yes. The criminal will do too much," Reggie sighed.

"Then Faulks came. He tumbled into us and hit out, silly ass. I heard Sally go down and I let him have it. Confound him."

Sally smiled at him affectionately.

"Oh yes, it's devilish funny, isn't it?" cried Tom Beach. "Good God, Cosdon, you're not fit to be at large. A nice thing you've let me in for."

"Well, you've all been very ingenious," said Reggie. "Thanks for a very jolly evening. May I have some breakfast?" There was a silence which could be felt.

"Mr. Fortune," said Sally, "that awful brooch is gone."

"Yes, that's where we slipped up," said Cosdon. "Sally must have dropped it when that fool knocked her out. I went out last night to hunt for it and it wasn't there."

"Really?"

Reggie's tone was sardonic and Cosdon flushed at it. "What do you mean?"

"Well, somebody found it, I suppose. That's the working hypothesis."

He reduced them to the dismal condition in which he found them. "There you are!" Colonel Beach cried. "Some one of the servants saw the beastly thing and thought there was a chance to steal it. It's a ghastly business. I'll have to go through them for it and catch some poor devil who would have gone straight enough if you hadn't played the fool. It's not fair, confound it."

There was a tap at the door. Mrs. Faulks was asking if the Colonel would speak to her. The Colonel groaned and went out.

"Do you mind if I have some breakfast, Mrs. Beach?" said Reggie plaintively.

They seemed to think him heartless but offered no impediment. A dejected company slunk downstairs. It occurred to Reggie, always a just man, that Sam also might be hungry and he ran out to take him off guard.

When he came back to the breakfast-room, he found that Faulks had joined the party. It was clear that no one had dared to tell him the truth. They were gazing in fascinated horror at the many colours which swelled about his right eye, and his scowl was terrible.

"Hallo, Faulks! Stout fellow," said Reggie, brightly. "How's the head?"

Mr. Faulks turned the scowl on him. Mr. Faulks found his head very painful. He had had practically no sleep. He feared some serious injury to the nerves. He must see a doctor. And his tone implied that as a doctor and a man Reggie was contemptible.

Reggie served himself generously with bacon and mushrooms and began to eat. No one else was eating but Mr. Faulks. He, in a domineering manner, smote boiled eggs. The others played with food like passengers in a rolling ship.

The door was opened. The austere shape of Mrs. Faulks stalked in and behind her Tom Beach slunk to his place. Mrs. Faulks's compressed face wore a look of triumph.

Sally half rose from her chair. "Oh, Mrs. Faulks," she cried, "have you found your rubies?"

"Really!" said Mrs. Faulks with a freezing smile. "No, Miss Winslow, I have not found my rubies."

"What are you going to do about it?"

Mrs. Faulks stared at her. "I imagine there is only one thing to be done. I have desired Colonel Beach to send for the police. I should have thought that was obvious."

"Oh, Tom, you mustn't!" Sally cried.

"Really! My dear, you don't realize what you're saying."

"Yes, I do. You don't understand, Mrs. Faulks; you see it was like this— —" and out it all came with the Colonel trying to stop it in confused exclamations, and Mrs. Faulks and her heavy son sinking deeper and deeper into stupefaction.

"The whole affair was a practical joke?" said Faulks thickly.

"That's the idea, old thing," Cosdon assured him.

"Yes, yes, don't you see it?" Sally giggled.

"I never heard anything so disgraceful," Faulks pronounced.

"I say, go easy," Cosdon cried.

Mrs. Faulks had become pale. "Am I expected to believe this?" she looked from Tom to Alice.

"Oh, Mrs. Faulks, I am so sorry," Alice Beach said. "It was too bad. And it's really all my fault."

"I—I—you say you stole my rubies?" Mrs. Faulks turned upon Sally.

"Come, come, the child took them for a joke," Colonel Beach protested.

"I took them, yes-and then I lost them. I'm most awfully sorry about that."

"Are you indeed. Am I to believe this tale, Colonel Beach? Then pray who stole my diamond necklace?"

She produced an awful silence. She seemed proud of it, and in a fascination of horror the conspirators stared at her.

"Diamond necklace!" Sally cried. "I never saw it."

"My necklace is gone. I don't profess to understand the ideas of joking in this house. But my necklace is gone."

"Oh, my lord," said Cosdon. "That's torn it."

"The snowball!" Alice gasped. "It is a snowball. Everything gets in something else."

"Really!" said Mrs. Faulks (her one expletive). "I do not understand you."

Reggie arose and cut himself a large portion of cold beef.

"If this was a practical joke," said the solemn voice of Faulks, "who struck me?"

"That was me, old thing," Cosdon smiled upon him.

"But strictly speakin'," said Reggie as he came back and took more toast, "that's irrelevant."

"Colonel Beach!" Mrs. Faulks commanded the wretched man's attention, "what do you propose to do?"

"We shall have to have the police," he groaned.

"Oh, yes, it's a case for the police," said Reggie cheerfully. "Have you a telegraph form, Colonel?"

"It's all right, Fortune, thanks. I'll telephone."

"Yes, encourage local talent. But I would like to send a wire to Scotland Yard."

"Scotland Yard!" Mrs. Faulks was impressed. Mrs. Faulks smiled on him.

"Well, you know, there are points about your case, Mrs. Faulks. I think they would be interested."

Like one handing his own death warrant, Colonel Beach put down some telegraph forms. Reggie pulled out his pencil, laid it down again and took some marmalade. "Valuable necklace, of course, Mrs. Faulks?" he said blandly. "Quite so. The one you wore the night before last? I remember. I remember." He described it. Mrs. Faulks approved and elaborated his description. "That's very clear. Are your jewels insured? Yes, well that is a certain consolation." He adjusted his pencil and wrote. "I think this will meet the case." He gave the telegram to Mrs. Faulks.

Mrs. Faulks read it, Mrs. Faulks seemed unable to understand. She continued to gaze at it, and the wondering company saw her grow red to the frozen coils of her hair.

Reggie was making notes on another telegraph form. He read out slowly a precise description of the lost necklace. "That's it, then," he said. "By the way, who are you insured with?"

Mrs. Faulks glared at him. "I suppose this is another joke."

"No," Reggie shook his head. "This has gone beyond a joke."

"Where is my brooch, then? Who has my brooch?"

"I have," said Reggie. He pulled it out of his pocket and laid it on her plate. "I found the brooch in the passage. I didn't find the necklace, Mrs. Faulks. So I should like to send that telegram."

"You will do nothing of the kind. I won't have anything done. The whole affair is disgraceful, perfectly disgraceful. I forbid you to interfere. Do you understand, I forbid it? Colonel Beach! It is impossible for me to stay in your house after the way in which you have allowed me to be treated. Please order the car."

She stalked out of the room.

"Fortune!" said Faulks thunderously. "Will you kindly explain yourself?"

"I don't think I need explaining. But you might ask your mother. She kept the telegram." And to his mother Mr. Faulks fled.

"Good God, Fortune, what have you done?" Tom Beach groaned.

"Not a nice woman," said Reggie sadly. "Not really a nice woman." He stood up and sought the fire and lit a cigar and sighed relief.

"Mr. Fortune, what was in that telegram?" Sally cried.

Reggie sat down on the cushioned fender. "I don't think you're really a good little girl, you know," he shook his head at her and surveyed the company. "Broadly speakin' you ought all to be ashamed of yourselves. Except the Colonel."

"Please, Mr. Fortune, I'll never do it again," said Alice plaintively. "Tom ——" she sat on the arm of her husband's chair and caressed him.

"All right, all right," he submitted. "But I say, Fortune, what am I to do about Mrs. Faulks?"

"She's done all there is to do. No, not a nice woman."

Sally held out her small hands. "Please! What did you say in that telegram?"

" 'Lomas, Scotland Yard. Jewel robbery Colonel Beach's house curious features tell post office stop delivery registered packet posted Cranston this morning nine examine contents Reginald Fortune Cranston Regis.' "

"I don't understand."

"She did. Sorry to meddle with anyone in your house. Colonel. But she would have it. You won't have any trouble."

"But what's the woman done?" the Colonel cried.

"Well, you know, she's been led into temptation. When she thought burglars had taken her brooch it seemed to her that she might as well recover from the insurance people for something else too. That's the worst of playing at crime, Mrs. Beach. You never know who won't take it seriously. What made me cast an eye at Mrs. Faulks was her saying last night that she wasn't sure whether she had lost anything else. I can't imagine Mrs. Faulks not sure about anything. She's sure she's an injured woman now. And I'll swear she always has an inventory of all her jeweller's shop in her head."

"She has," said Alice Beach pathetically. "You should hear her talk of her jewels."

"Heaven forbid. But you see, Miss Winslow, it's the old story, you criminals always try to be too clever. She thought it wouldn't be enough to say she'd lost her diamonds. She wanted them well out of the way so that the police could search and not find them. So she scurried off to the post office and sent them away in a registered packet. Thus, as you criminals will, underratin' the intelligence of the simple policeman. My man Sam was looking out to see if anyone did anything unusual this morning and he observed Mrs. Faulks's manœuvres at the post office ——"

"And you had her cold!" Cosdon cried.

"Yes. Yes, a sad story."

"She didn't really mean any harm," said Sally. "Did she, Mr. Fortune?"

Reggie looked at her sadly. "You're not a moral little girl, you know," he said.

CASE VI

THE LEADING LADY

MR. REGINALD FORTUNE sent his punt along at the rate of knots. From the cushions the Chief of the Criminal Investigation Department protested. "Why this wanton display of skill? Why so strenuous?"

"It's good for the figure, Lomas."

"Have you a figure?" said Lomas bitterly. It is to be confessed that a certain solidity distinguishes Reggie Fortune. Years of service as the scientific adviser of Scotland Yard have not marred the pink and white of his cherubic face, but they have brought weight to a body never svelte.

Mr. Fortune let the punt drift. "That's vulgar abuse. What's the matter, old thing?"

"I dislike your horrible competence. Is there anything you can't do?"

"I don't think so," said Mr. Fortune modestly. "Jack of all trades and master of none. That is why I am a specialist."

The Hon. Sidney Lomas sat up. "Secondly, I resent your hurry to get rid of me. Thirdly, as I am going up to London to work and you are going back in this punt to do nothing, I should like to annoy you. Fourthly and lastly I know that I shan't, and that embitters me. Does anything ever annoy you, Fortune?"

"Only work. Only the perverse criminal."

Lomas groaned. "All criminals are perverse."

"Oh, I wouldn't say that. Most crime is a natural product."

"Of course fools are natural," said Lomas irritably. "The most natural of all animals. And if there were no fools—I shouldn't spend the summer at Scotland Yard."

"Well, many criminals are weak in the head."

"That's why a policeman's life is not a happy one."

"But most of 'em are a natural product. Opportunity makes the thief or what not-and there but for the grace of God go I. Circumstances lead a fellow into temptation."

"Yes. I've wanted to do murder myself. But even with you I have hitherto refrained. There's always a kink in the criminal's mind before he goes wrong. Good Gad!" He dropped his voice. "Did you see her?"

Mr. Fortune reproved him. "You're so susceptible, Lomas. Control yourself. Think of my reputation. I am known in these parts."

"Who is she? Lady Macbeth?"

"My dear fellow! Oh, my dear fellow! I thought you were a student of the drama. She's not tragic. She's comedy and domestic pathos. Tea and tears. It was Rose Darcourt."

"Good Gad!" said Lomas once more. "She looked like Lady Macbeth after the murder."

Reggie glanced over his shoulder. From the shade of the veranda of the boat-house a white face stared at him. It seemed to become aware of him and fled. "Indigestion perhaps," he said. "It does feel like remorse. Or have you been trifling with her affections, Lomas?"

"I wouldn't dare. Do you know her? She looks a nice young woman for a quiet tea-party. Passion and poison for two."

"It's the physique, you know," said Mr. Fortune sadly. "When they're long and sinuous and dark they will be intense. That's the etiquette of the profession. But it's spoiling her comedy. She takes everything in spasms now and she used to be quite restful."

"Some silly fool probably told her she was a great actress," Lomas suggested.

Mr. Fortune did not answer. He was steering the punt to the bank. As it slid by the rushes he stooped and picked out of the water a large silk bag. This he put down at Lomas's feet, and saying, "Who's the owner of this pretty thing?" once more drove the punt on at the rate of knots.

Lomas produced from the bag a powder-puff, three gold hair-pins and two handkerchiefs. "The police have evidence of great importance," he announced, "and immediate developments are expected. S. Sheridan is the culprit, Fortune."

"Sylvia Sheridan?" Reggie laughed. "You know we're out of a paragraph in a picture paper. 'On the river this week-end all the stars of the stage were shining. Miss Rose Darcourt was looking like Juliet on the balcony of her charming boat-house and I saw Miss Sylvia Sheridan's bag floating sweetly down stream. Bags are worn bigger than ever this year. Miss Sheridan has always been famous for her bags. But this was really dinky!' "

At the bridge he put Lomas into his car and strolled up to leave Miss Sheridan's bag at the police-station.

The sergeant was respectfully affable (Mr. Fortune is much petted by subordinates) and it took some time to reach the bag. When Ascot and the early peas and the sergeant's daughter's young man had been critically estimated, Mr. Fortune said that he was only calling on the lost property department to leave a lady's bag. "I just picked it out of the river," Reggie explained. "No value to anybody but the owner. Seems to belong to Miss Sylvia Sheridan. She's a house down here, hasn't she? You might let her know."

The sergeant stared at Mr. Fortune and breathed hard. "What makes you say that, sir?"

"Say what?"

"Beg pardon, sir. You'd better see the inspector." And the sergeant tumbled out of the room.

The inspector was flurried. "Mr. Fortune? Very glad to see you, sir. Sort of providential your coming in like this. Won't you sit down, sir? This is a queer start. Where might you have found her bag, Mr. Fortune?"

"About a mile above the bridge," Reggie opened his eyes. "Against the reed bank below Miss Darcourt's boat-house."

Inspector Oxtoby whistled. "That's above Miss Sheridan's cottage." He looked knowing. "Things don't float upstream, Mr. Fortune."

"It's not usual. Why does that worry you?"

"Miss Sheridan's missing, Mr. Fortune. I've just had her housekeeper in giving information. Miss Sheridan went out last night and hasn't been seen since. Now you've picked up her bag in the river above her house. It's a queer start, isn't it?"

"But only a start," said Reggie gently. "We're not even sure the bag is hers. The handkerchiefs in it are marked S. Sheridan. But some women have a way of gleaning other women's handkerchiefs. Her housekeeper ought to know her bag. Did her housekeeper know why she went out?"

"No, sir. That's one of the things that rattled her. Miss Sheridan went out after dinner alone, walking. They thought she was in the garden and went to bed. In the morning she wasn't in the house. She wasn't in the garden either."

"And that's that," said Reggie. "Better let them know at Scotland Yard. They like work." And he rose to go. It was plain that he had disappointed Inspector Oxtoby, who asked rather plaintively if there was anything Mr. Fortune could suggest. "I should ask her friends, you know," said Mr. Fortune, wandering dreamily to the door. "I should have a look at her house. There may be something in it," and he left the inspector gaping.

Reggie Fortune is one of the few people in England who like going to the theatre. The others, as you must have noticed, like this kind of play or that. Mr. Fortune has an impartial and curious mind and tries everything. He had therefore formed opinions of Sylvia Sheridan and Rose Darcourt which are not commonly held. For he was unable to take either of them seriously. This hampered him, and he calls the case one of his failures.

On the next morning he came back from bathing at the lasher to hear that the telephone had called him. He took his car to Scotland Yard and was received by Superintendent Bell. That massive man was even heavier than usual. "You'll not be pleased with me, Mr. Fortune — —" he began.

"If you look at me like that I shall cry. Two hours ago I was in nice deep bubbly water. And you bring me up to this oven of a town and make me think you're a headmaster with the gout and I've been a rude little boy."

"Mr. Lomas said not to trouble you," the Superintendent mourned. "But I put it to him you'd not wish to be out of it, Mr. Fortune."

"Damn it, Bell, don't appeal to my better nature. That's infuriating."

"It's this Sheridan case, sir. Miss Sheridan's vanished."

"Well, I haven't run away with her. She smiles too much. I couldn't bear it."

"She's gone, sir," Bell said heavily. "She was to have signed her contract as leading lady in Mr. Mark Woodcote's new play. That was yesterday. She didn't come. They had no word from her. And yesterday her servants gave information she had disappeared——"

"I know. I was there. So she hasn't turned up yet?"

"No, sir. And Mr. Lomas and you, you found her bag in the river. That was her bag."

"Well, well." said Reggie. "And what's the Criminal Investigation Department going to do about it?"

"Where's she gone, Mr. Fortune? She didn't take her car. She's not been seen at Stanton station. She's not at her flat in town. She's not with any of her friends."

"The world is wide," Reggie murmured.

"And the river's pretty deep, Mr. Fortune."

At this point Lomas came in. He beamed upon them both, he patted Bell's large shoulder, he came to Reggie Fortune. "My dear fellow! Here already! 'Duty, stern daughter of the voice of God,' what? How noble-and how good for you!"

Reggie looked from his jauntiness to the gloom of Bell. "Tragedy and comedy, aren't you?" he said. "And very well done, too. But it's a little confusing to the scientific mind."

"Well, what do you make of it?" Lomas dropped into a chair and lit a cigarette. "Bell's out for blood. An Actress's Tragedy. Mystery of the Thames. Murder or Suicide? That sort of thing. But it seems to me it has all the engaging air of an advertisement."

"Only it isn't advertised, sir," said Bell. "Twenty-four hours and more since she was reported missing, and not a word in the papers yet. That don't look like a stunt. It looks more like somebody was keeping things quiet."

"Yes. Yes, you take that trick, Bell," Reggie nodded. "Who is this remarkable manager that don't tell all the newspapers when his leading lady's missing?"

"Mr. Montgomery Eagle, sir."

"But he runs straight," said Reggie.

"Oh Lord, yes," Lomas laughed. "Quite a good fellow. Bell is so melodramatic in the hot weather. I don't think Eagle is pulling my leg. I suspect it's the lady who is out for a little free advertisement. To be reported missing-that is a sure card. On the placards, in the headlines, unlimited space in all the papers. Wait and see, Bell. The delay means nothing. She couldn't tell her Press agent to send in news of her disappearance. It wouldn't be artistic."

Superintendent Bell looked at him compassionately. "And I'm sure I hope you're right, sir," he said. "But it don't look that way to me. If she wanted to disappear for a joke why did she go and do it like this? These young ladies on the stage, they value their comforts. She goes off walking at night with nothing but what she stood up in. If you ask me to believe she meant to do the vanishing act when she went out of her house, I can't see how it's likely."

"Strictly speakin'," said Reggie, "nothing's likely. Why did she go out, Bell? To keep an appointment with her murderer?"

"I don't see my way, sir. I own it. But there's her garden goes down to the river-suppose she just tumbled into the water-she might be there now."

"The bag," said Reggie dreamily. "The bag, Bell. It didn't float upstream, and yet we found it above her garden. She couldn't have been walking along the bank. The towpath is the other side. The bag came into the river from a boat-or from the grounds of another house."

Lomas laughed. "My dear Fortune, I like your earnest simplicity. It's a new side to your character and full of charm. I quite agree the bag is interesting. I think it's conclusive. A neat and pretty touch. The little lady threw it into the river to give her disappearance glamour."

"Rather well thrown," said Reggie. "Say a quarter of a mile. Hefty damsel."

"Oh, my dear fellow, she may have taken a boat, she may have crossed and walked up the towpath."

"Just to get her bag into the river above her house? Why would she want to put it in above her house? She couldn't be sure that it would stay there. It might have sunk. It might have drifted a mile farther."

Lomas shrugged. "Well, as you say. But we don't know that the bag was lost that night at all. She may have dropped it out of a boat any time and anywhere."

"Yes, but plenty of boats go up and down that reach. And we found it bright and early the morning after she vanished. Why didn't anybody else find it before? I rather fancy it wasn't there, Lomas."

"What's your theory, Mr. Fortune?" said Bell eagerly.

"My dear fellow! Oh, my dear fellow! I don't know the lady."

"They say she's a sportive maiden," Lomas smiled. "I'll wager you'll have a run for your money, Bell."

Reggie Fortune considered him severely. "I don't think it's a race to bet on, Lomas, old thing."

It was about this time that Mr. Montgomery Eagle's name was brought in. "Will you see him, Mr. Lomas?" Bell said anxiously.

"Oh Lord, no. I have something else to do. Make him talk, that's all you want."

The Superintendent turned a bovine but pathetic gaze on Reggie. "I think so," said Mr. Fortune. "There are points, Bell."

Superintendent Bell arranged himself at the table, a large solemn creature, born to inspire confidence. Mr. Fortune dragged an easy chair to the window and sat on the small of his back and thus disposed might have been taken for an undergraduate weary of the world.

Mr. Montgomery Eagle brought another man with him. They both exhibited signs of uneasiness. Mr. Eagle, whose physical charms, manner and dress suggest a butler off duty, wrung his hands and asked if the Superintendent had any news. The Superintendent asked Mr. Eagle to sit down. "Er, thank you. Er-you're very good. May I—this is Mr. Woodcote-the-er-author of the play Miss Sheridan was to-the-play I—er-hope to-very anxious to know if you———"

"Naturally," said the Superintendent. "Pleased to meet you, Mr. Woodcote." The dramatist smiled nervously. He was still young enough to show an awkward simplicity of manner, but his pleasant dark face had signs of energy and some ability. "We're rather interested in your case. Now what have you got to tell us?"

"I?" said Woodcote. "Well, I hoped you were going to tell us something."

"We've heard nothing at all," said Eagle. "Absolutely nothing. Er-it's—er-very distressing-er-serious matter for us-er-whole production held up-er-this poor lady-most distressing."

"Quite, quite," Reggie murmured from his chair, and the two stared at him.

"The fact is," said Superintendent Bell heavily, "we can find no one who has seen Miss Sheridan since she left her house. We're where we were yesterday, gentlemen. Are you?"

"Absolutely," said Eagle.

"First question-did she leave her house?" Reggie murmured. "Second question-why did she leave her house?" He sat up with a jerk. "I wonder. Do you know anything about that?"

Eagle gaped at him. "Did she leave her house?" Woodcote cried. "That's not doubtful, is it? She's not there."

"Well, I like to begin at the beginning," said Reggie gently.

"The local men have been over the house, Mr. Fortune," Bell stared at him.

"I suppose they wouldn't overlook her," Woodcote laughed.

"Second question-why did she leave it? You see, we don't know the lady and I suppose you do. Had she any friends who were-intimate?"

"What are you suggesting?" Woodcote cried.

"I don't know. Do you? Is there anyone she liked-or anyone she didn't like?"

"I must say," —Eagle was emphatic in jerks —"never heard a word said-er-against Miss Sheridan-er-very highest reputation."

"If you have any suspicions let's have it out, sir," Woodcote cried.

"My dear fellow! Oh, my dear fellow!" Reggie protested. "It's the case is suspicious, not me. The primary hypothesis is that something made Miss Sheridan vanish. I'm askin' you what it was."

The manager looked at the dramatist. The dramatist looked at Mr. Fortune. "What is it you suspect, then?" he said.

"What does take a lady out alone after dinner?" said Reggie. "I wonder."

"We don't know that she went out of the garden, sir," Bell admonished him.

Reggie lit a cigar. "Think there was a murderer waiting in the garden?" he said as he puffed. "Think she was feeling suicidal? Well, it's always possible."

"Good God!" said Eagle.

"You're rather brutal, sir," Woodcote grew pale.

"You don't like those ideas? Well, what's yours?" They were silent. "Has it ever occurred to you somebody might have annoyed Miss Sheridan?" Mr. Montgomery Eagle became of a crimson colour. "Yes, think it over," said Reggie cheerfully. "If there was somebody she wanted to take it out of——" he smiled and blew smoke rings.

"I don't know what you mean," Woodcote stared at him.

"Really? It's quite simple. Had anything happened lately to make Miss Sheridan annoyed with anybody?"

"I'm bound to say, sir," Eagle broke out, "there was a —a question about her part. She was to play lead in Mr. Woodcote's new comedy. Well-er—I can't deny-er-Miss Darcourt's been with me before. Miss Darcourt-she was-well, I had-er-representations from her the part ought to be hers. I —er —I'm afraid Miss Sheridan did come to hear of this."

"Rose Darcourt couldn't play it," said the author fiercely. "She couldn't touch it."

"No, no. I don't suggest she could-er-not at all-but it was an unpleasant situation. Miss Sheridan was annoyed ——"

"Miss Sheridan was annoyed with Miss Darcourt and Miss Darcourt was annoyed with Miss Sheridan. And Miss Sheridan goes out alone at night by the river and in the river we find her bag. That's the case, then. Well, well."

"Do you mean that Rose Darcourt murdered her?" Woodcote frowned at him.

"My dear fellow, you are in such a hurry. I mean that I could bear to know a little more about Miss Darcourt's emotions. Do you think you could find out if she still wants to play this great part?"

"She may want," said Woodcote bitterly. "She can go on wanting."

"In point of fact," said Eagle. "I —er —I had a letter this morning. She tells me-er-she wouldn't consider acting in-er-in Mr. Woodcote's play. She-er-says I misunderstood her. She never thought of it-er-doesn't care for Mr. Woodcote's work."

Mr. Woodcote flushed. "That does worry me," said he.

"And that's that." Reggie stood up.

Whereon Superintendent Bell with careful official assurances got rid of them. They seemed surprised.

"That's done it, sir," said Bell. Reggie did not answer. He was cooing to a pigeon on the window-sill. "You've got it out of them. We'll be looking after this Rose Darcourt."

"They don't like her, do they?" Reggie murmured. "Well, well. They do enjoy their little emotions." He laughed suddenly. "Let's tell Lomas."

That sprightly man was reading an evening paper. He flung it at Bell's head. "There you are. Six-inch headlines. 'Famous Actress Vanishes.' And now I do hope we shan't be long. I wonder how she'll manage her resurrection. Was she kidnapped by a Bolshevik submarine? U-boat in Boulter's Lock. That would be a good stunt. And rescued by an aeroplane. She might come down on the course at Ascot."

"He can't take her seriously, Bell," said Reggie. "It's the other one who has his heart. Who ever loved that loved not at first sight? She captured him at a glance."

Bell was shocked and bewildered. "What the deuce do you mean?" said Lomas.

"Lady Macbeth by the river. You know how she fascinated you."

"Rose Darcourt?" Lomas cried. "Good Gad!"

"The morning after Sylvia Sheridan vanished, Rose Darcourt was looking unwell by the river and Sylvia Sheridan's bag was found in the river just below Rose Darcourt's house. Now the manager and the playwright tell us Rose has been trying to get the part which was earmarked for Sylvia, and Sylvia was cross about it. Since Sylvia vanished Rose has pitched in a letter to say she wouldn't look at the part or the play. Consider your verdict."

"There it is, sir, and an ugly business," said Bell with a certain satisfaction. "These stage folk, they're not wholesome."

"My dear old Bell," Reggie chuckled.

"Good Gad!" said Lomas, and burst out laughing. "But it's preposterous. It's a novelette. The two leading ladies quarrel-and they meet by moonlight alone on the banks of the murmuring stream-and pull caps-and what happened next? Did Rose pitch Sylvia into the dark and deadly water or Sylvia commit suicide in her anguish? Damme, Bell, you'd better make a film of it."

"I don't know what you make of it, sir," said Bell with stolid indignation. "But I've advised the local people to drag the river. And I suggest it's time we had a man or two looking after this Miss Darcourt."

"Good Gad!" said Lomas again. "And what do you suggest. Fortune? Do you want to arrest her and put her on the rack? Or will it be enough to examine her body for Sylvia's finger-prints? If we are to make fools of ourselves, let's do it handsomely."

"It seems to me we look fools enough as it is," Bell growled.

"This is a very painful scene," Reggie said gently. "Your little hands were never made to scratch each other's eyes."

"What do you want to do?" Lomas turned on him.

"Well, it's not much in my way. I like a corpse and you haven't a corpse for me. And I don't feel that I know these good people. They seem muddled to me. It's all muddled. I fancy they don't know where they are. And there's something we haven't got, Lomas old thing. I should look about."

"I'm going to look about," said Lomas with decision. "But I'm going to look for Sylvia Sheridan's friends-not her wicked rivals. I resent being used as an actress's advertisement."

Reggie shook his head. "You will be so respectable, Lomas my child. It hampers you."

"Well, go and drag the river," said Lomas with a shrug, "and see who finds her first."

Mr. Fortune, who has a gentle nature, does not like people to be cross to him. This was his defence when Lomas subsequently complained of his independent action. He went to lunch and afterwards returned to his house by the river.

Swaying in a hammock under the syringa he considered the Sheridan case without prejudice, and drowsily came to the conclusion that he believed in nothing and nobody. He was not satisfied with the bag, he was not satisfied with the pallid woe of Rose Darcourt, he was not satisfied with the manager and the playwright, he was by no means satisfied with the flippancy of Lomas and the grim zeal of Bell. It appeared to him that all were unreasonable. He worked upon his memories of Rose Darcourt and Sylvia Sheridan and found no help therein. The two ladies, though competent upon the stage and at times agreeable, were to him commonplace. And whatever the case was, it was not that. He could not relate them to the floating bag, and the story of jealousy and the disappearance. "This thing's all out of joint," he sighed, "and I don't think the airy Lomas or the gloomy Bell is the man to put it right. Why will people have theories? And at their time of life too! It's not decent." He rang (in his immoral garden you can ring from the pergola and ring from the hammocks and the lawn) for his chauffeur and factotum, Sam.

Mr. Samuel Smith was born a small and perky Cockney. He is, according to Reggie, a middle-class chauffeur but otherwise a lad of parts, having a peculiarly neat hand with photography and wine. But a capacity for being all things to all men was what first recommended him. "Sam," said Mr. Fortune, "do you go much into society?"

"Meaning the locals, sir?"

"That was the idea."

"Well, sir, they're not brainy. Too much o' the *nouveau riche*."

"It's a hard world, Sam. I want to know about Miss Darcourt's servants. I wouldn't mind knowing about Miss Sheridan's servants. They ought to be talking things over. Somebody may be saying something interesting-or doing something."

"I've got it, sir. Can do."

Mr. Fortune sighed happily and went to sleep.

For the next few days he was occupied with a number of new roses which chose to come into flower together. It was reported among his servants that Mr. Fortune sat by these bushes and held their hands. And meanwhile the papers gave much space to Miss Sylvia Sheridan, describing in vivid detail how the river was being dragged for her, and how her corpse had been discovered at Bradford and how she had been arrested while bathing (mixed) at Ilfracombe and seen on a flapper's bracket in Hampstead.

Mr. Fortune, engaged upon a minute comparison of the shades of tawny red in five different but exquisite roses, was disturbed by Superintendent Bell. He looked up at that square and gloomy visage and shook his head. "You disturb me. I have my own troubles, Bell. Darlings, aren't they?" He made a caressing gesture over his roses. "But I can't make up my mind which is the one I really love. Go away, Bell. Your complexion annoys them."

"We haven't found her, sir," said Bell heavily. "She's not in the river." Reggie dropped into a long chair and, watching him with dreamy eyes, filled a pipe. Bell glowered. "I thought you were going to say, 'I told you so.' "

Reggie smiled. "I don't remember that I told you anything."

"That was about the size of it, sir," Bell reproached him.

"Well, I thought it was possible the body was in the river. But not probable."

"Nothing's probable that I can see. Roses are a bit simpler, aren't they, sir?"

"Simpler!" Reggie cried. "You're no gardener. You should take it up, Bell. It develops the finer feelings. Now, don't be cross again. I can't bear it. I haven't forgotten your horrible case. Nothing's probable, as you say. But one or two things are certain all the same. Sylvia Sheridan's servants have nothing up their sleeves. They're as lost as you are. They are being quite natural. But Rose Darcourt has a chauffeur who interests me. He is a convivial animal and his pub is the 'Dog and Duck.' But he hasn't been at the 'Dog and Duck' since Sylvia vanished. The 'Dog and Duck' is surprised at him. Also he has been hanging about Sylvia's house. He has suddenly begun an affair with her parlourmaid. He seems to have a deuce of a lot of time on his hands. Rose Darcourt don't show. She's reported ill. And the reputation of the chauffeur is that he's always been very free and easy with his mistress."

Bell grunted and meditated and Reggie pushed a cigar-case across to help his meditations. "Well, sir, it sounds queer as you put it. But it might be explained easy. And that's what Mr. Lomas says about the whole case. Maybe he's right." The thought plunged the Superintendent into deeper gloom.

"What a horrible idea," said Reggie. "My dear fellow, don't be so despondent. I've been waiting for you to take me to the parlourmaid. I want a chaperon."

Inspector Oxtoby in plain clothes, Superintendent Bell in clothes still plainer and Mr. Fortune in flannels conducted an examination of that frightened damsel, who was by turns impudent and plaintive, till soothed by Mr. Fortune's benignity. It then emerged that she was not walking out with Mr. Loveday the chauffeur: nothing of the kind: only Mr. Loveday had been attentive.

"And very natural, too," Reggie murmured. "But why has he only just begun?"

The parlourmaid was startled. They had had a many fellows round the house since mistress went off. She smiled. It was implied that others beside the chauffeur had remarked her charms.

"And Mr. Loveday never came before? Does he ask after your mistress?"

"Well, of course he always wants to know if she's been heard of. It's only civil, sir." She stopped and stared at Reggie. "I suppose he does talk a deal about the mistress," she said slowly.

"When he ought to be talking about you," Reggie murmured.

The parlourmaid looked frightened. "But it's as if he was always expecting some news of her," she protested.

"Oh, is it!" said Inspector Oxtoby, and Reggie frowned at him.

"Yes, it is!" she cried. "And I don't care what you say. And a good mistress she was"—she began to weep again, and was incoherent.

"I'm sure she was," Reggie said, "and you're fond of her. That's why we're here, you know. You want to help her, don't you? When was Mr. Loveday going to meet you again?"

Through sobs it was stated that Mr. Loveday had said he would be by the little gate at his usual time that night.

"Well, I don't want you to see him, Gladys," said Reggie gently. "You're to stay indoors like a good girl. Don't say anything to anybody and you'll be all right."

On that they left her, and Reggie, taking Bell's arm as they crossed the garden, murmured, "I like Gladys. She's a pleasant shape. This job's opening out, Bell, isn't it?"

"It beats me," said Bell. "What's the fellow after?"

"He knows something," said Oxtoby.

"And he's not quite sure what he knows," said Reggie. "Well, well. An early dinner is indicated. It's a hard world. Come and dine with me."

That night as it grew dark the chauffeur stood by the little gate of Sylvia Sheridan's garden, an object of interest to three men behind a laurel hedge. He waited some time in vain. He lit a cigarette and exhibited for a moment a large flat face. He waited longer, opened the gate and approached the back of the house.

"Better take him now," said Reggie. "Loitering with intent. I'll go down to the station."

Inspector Oxtoby, with Bell in support, closed upon the man in the kitchen garden.

In the little office at Stanton police-station Albert Edward Loveday was charged with loitering about Miss Sheridan's house with intent to commit a felony. He was loudly indignant, protesting that he had only gone to see his girl. He was told that he could say all that to the magistrates, and was removed still noisy.

Mr. Fortune came out of the shadow. "I don't take to Albert Edward," he said. "I fear he's a bit of a bully."

Bell nodded. "That's his measure, sir. A chap generally shows what he's made of when you get him in the charge room. I never could understand that. You'd think any fellow with a head on him would take care to hide what sort he is here. But they don't seem as if they could help themselves."

"Most of the fellows you get in the charge room haven't heads. I doubt if Albert Edward has. He looks as if he hadn't thought things out."

Inspector Oxtoby came back in a hurry. "My oath, Mr. Fortune, you've put us on the right man," he said. "Look what the beggar had on him." It was a small gold cigarette-case. It bore the monogram S.S., and inside was engraved "Sylvia from Bingo."

"That's done him in," said Bell. "Any explanation?"

"He wouldn't say a word. Barring that he cursed freely. No, Mr. Albert Edward Loveday wants to see his solicitor. He knows something."

"Yes. Yes, I wonder what it is?" Reggie murmured.

"He had some pawn-tickets for jewellery too. Pretty heavy stuff. We'll have to follow that up. And a hundred and fifty quid-some clean notes, some deuced dirty."

Bell laughed grimly. "He's done himself proud, hasn't he?"

"Some clean, some dirty," Reggie repeated. "He got the dirty ones from the pawnbroker. Where did he get the clean ones? Still several unknown quantities in the equation."

"How's that, sir?" said Inspector Oxtoby.

"Well, there's the body, for instance," said Reggie mildly. "We lack the body. You know, I think we might ask Miss Darcourt to say a few words. Send a man up in a car to tell her she's wanted at the police-station, because her chauffeur has been arrested. I should think she'll come."

"That's the stuff!" Inspector Oxtoby chuckled and set about it.

"You always had a notion she knew something, sir," said Bell reverently.

"I wonder," Reggie murmured.

She did come. The little room seemed suddenly crowded, so large was the gold pattern on her black cloak, so complex her sinuous movements, as she glided in and sat down. She smiled at them, and certainly she had been handsome. From a white face dark eyes glittered, very big eyes, all pupil. "Oh, my aunt," said Reggie to himself, "drugged."

"Miss Rose Darcourt?" Inspector Oxtoby's pen scratched. "Thank you, madam. Your chauffeur Albert Edward Loveday (that's right?) has been arrested loitering about Miss Sheridan's house. He was found in possession of Miss Sheridan's gold cigarette-case. Can you explain that?"

"I? Why should I explain it? I know nothing about it."

"The man is in your service, madam."

"Yes, and he is a very good chauffeur. What then? Why should you arrest him?" She talked very fast. "I don't understand it at all. I don't understand what you want me to say."

"Only the truth," said Reggie gently out of the shadow.

"What do you mean by the truth? I know nothing about what he had. I can't imagine, I can't conceive"—her voice went up high—"how he could have Miss Sheridan's cigarette-case. If he really had."

"Oh, he had it all right," said Inspector Oxtoby.

"Why, then perhaps she gave it him." She laughed so suddenly that the men looked at each other. "Have you asked him? What did he say? I know nothing about Miss Sheridan."

"You can tell us nothing?" said Reggie.

"What should I tell you?" she cried.

There was silence but for the scratching of the Inspector's pen. "Very good, madam," he said. "You have no explanation. I had better tell you the case will go into court. Thank you for coming. Would you like to have the car back?"

"What has Loveday said?" She leaned forward.

"He's asked for his solicitor, madam. That's all."

"What is this charge, then?"

The Inspector smiled. "That's as may be, madam."

"Can I see him?"

"Not alone, I'm afraid, ma'am," said Bell.

"What?" she cried. "What do you mean?"

"The car'll take you back, ma'am."

She stared at him a long minute. "The car?" she started up. "I don't need your car. I'll not have it. I can go, can I?" she laughed.

Bell opened the door. "Phew!" he puffed as he closed it. "She looked murder, didn't she?"

"Nice young woman for a quiet tea-party," Reggie murmured. "I wonder. I wonder. I think I'll use that car."

As it drew out upon the bridge he saw the tall shape of Miss Darcourt ahead. She was going slowly. She stopped. She glanced behind her at the lights of the car. She climbed the parapet and was gone.

"Oh, damn!" said Mr. Fortune. "Stop the bus." He sprang out, looked down for a moment at the foam and the eddies and dived after her.

Some minutes afterwards he arrived at the bank with Miss Darcourt in tow and waddled out, dragging her after him without delicacy and swearing in gasps. She was in no case to protest. She did not hear. Mr. Fortune rolled her over and knelt beside her.

"What'll I do, sir? Can't I do something?" cried the chauffeur.

"Police-station," Reggie panted. "Bring down the Inspector or the Superintendent. Quick! Damn quick!" And he wrought with Miss Darcourt's body....

He looked up at the large shape of Superintendent Bell. "Suicide, sir?"

"Attempted suicide. She'll do, I think. Wrap her in every dam' thing you've got and take her to hospital quick."

"I know this game, sir," Bell said, and stooped and gathered the woman up: "you run along home."

"Run!" said Reggie. "My only aunt."

In the morning when he rang for his letters, "Superintendent Bell called, sir," said the maid. "About eight it was. He said I wasn't to waken you. He only wanted to tell you she was going on all right. And there's a message by telephone from Mr. Lomas. He says you should be at Paddington by twelve, car will meet you, very urgent. And to tell you he has the body."

"Oh, my Lord!" said Reggie. He sprang out of bed. Superintendent Bell was rung up and told to commit himself to nothing over Albert Edward Loveday and his mistress.

"Remanded for inquiries-that'll do for him, sir," said Bell's voice. "And she can wait. Hope you're all right, Mr. Fortune."

"I'm suffering from shock, Bell. Mr. Lomas is shocking me. He's begun to sit up and take notice."

Inadequately fed and melancholy, Mr. Fortune was borne into Paddington by a quarter-past twelve. He there beheld Lomas sitting in Lomas's car and regarding him with a satirical eye. Mr. Fortune entered the car in dignity and silence.

"My dear fellow, I hate to disappoint you," Lomas smiled. "You've done wonderfully well. Arrested a chauffeur, driven a lady to suicide-admirable. It is really your masterpiece. Art for art's sake in the grand style. You must find it horribly disappointing to act with a dull fellow like me."

"I do," said Mr. Fortune.

Lomas chuckled. "I know, I know. I can't help seeing it. And really I hate to spoil your work. But the plain fact is I've got the body."

"Well, well," said Mr. Fortune.

"And unfortunately—I really do sympathize with you-it isn't dead."

"When did I say it was?" said Mr. Fortune. "I said you hadn't a corpse for me-and you haven't got one now. I said it was all muddled-and so it is, a dam' muddle."

"Don't you want to know why the fair Sylvia left home?"

"Yes. Do you know, Lomas?"

"She's gone off with a man, my dear fellow," Lomas laughed.

"Well, well," said Reggie mildly. "And that's why the Darcourt's chauffeur had her cigarette-case in his pocket! And that's why the Darcourt jumped into the river when we asked her to explain! You make it all so clear, Lomas."

"Theft, I suppose, and fright." Lomas shrugged. "But we'll ask Sylvia."

"Where is she?"

"I had information of some one like her from a little place in the wilds of Suffolk. I sent a fellow down and he has no doubt it's the lady. She's been living there since she vanished, with a man."

"What man?"

"Not identified. Smith by name," said Lomas curtly. "You'd better ask her yourself, Fortune."

"Yes. There's quite a lot of things I'd like to ask her," said Reggie, and conversation languished. Even the elaborate lunch which Reggie insisted on eating in Colchester did not revive it, for Lomas was fretful at the delay. So at last, with Reggie somnolent and Lomas feverish, the car drew up at the ancient inn of the village of Baldon.

A young fellow who was drinking ginger-beer in the porch looked up and came to meet them. "She's done a bunk, sir," he said in a low voice. "She and her Mr. Smith went off half an hour ago. Some luggage in the car. Took the London road."

"My poor Lomas!" Reggie chuckled.

"Damme, we must have passed them on the road," Lomas cried. "Any idea why she went, Blakiston?"

"No, sir. The man went into Ipswich in their car this morning. Soon after he came back, they bolted together. I couldn't do anything, you know, sir."

"You're sure Mrs. Smith is Miss Sheridan?"

"I'd swear to her, sir."

"It's damned awkward," Lomas frowned. "Sorry, Fortune. We'd better be off back."

"I want my tea," said Reggie firmly, and got out: and vainly Lomas followed to protest that after the Colchester lunch he could want no more to eat for twenty-four hours. He was already negotiating for cream. "If it hadn't been for your confounded lunch we should have caught her," Lomas grumbled. "Now she's off into the blue again."

Reggie fell into the window seat and took up the local paper. "And where is he that knows?" he murmured. "From the great deep to the great deep she goes. But why? Assumin' for the sake of argument that she is our leading lady, why does she make this hurried exit?"

"How the devil should I know?"

Reggie smiled at him over the top of the papers. "This is a very interestin' journal," he remarked. "Do you know what it is, Lomas? It's the Ipswich evening paper with the 2.30 winner. Were you backing anything? No? Well, well. Not a race for a careful man. I read also that Miss Darcourt's chauffeur was brought up before the Stanton magistrates this morning and Miss Darcourt jumped into the river last night. It makes quite a lot of headlines. The Press is a great power, Lomas."

Lomas damned the Press.

"You're so old-fashioned," Reggie said sadly. "My child, don't you see? Mr. Smith went to Ipswich, Mr. Smith read the early evening paper and hustled back to tell Mrs. Smith, and Mrs. Smith felt that duty called her. Assuming that Mrs. Smith is our Sylvia, where would it call her? Back to Stanton, to clear up the mess."

"I suppose so," said Lomas drearily. "She can go to the devil for me."

"My dear chap, you do want your tea," said Reggie. Then Lomas swore.

It was late that night when a dusty car driven by Mr. Fortune approached the lights of Stanton. Mr. Fortune turned away from the bridge down a leafy byway and drew up with a jerk. Another car was standing by Miss Sheridan's gate. The man in it turned to stare. Reggie was already at his side. "Mr. Smith, I presume?" he said.

"Who the devil are you?" said a voice that seemed to him familiar.

The night was then rent by a scream, which resolved itself into a cry of "Thieves! Help, help! Police!" It came from the house.

Reggie made for the door and banged upon it. It was opened by an oldish woman in disarray. "We've got burglars," she cried. "Come in, sir, come in."

"Rather," said Mr. Fortune. "Where are they?"

"On the stair, sir. I hit him. I know I hit one. It give me such a turn."

Reggie ran upstairs. The light was on in the hall, but on the landing, in the shadow, he stumbled over something soft. He ran his hand along the wall for a switch and found it. What he saw was Sylvia Sheridan lying with blood upon her face.

"It's all right. You've only knocked out your mistress," he called over the stairs.

"Oh, my God!" the housekeeper gasped. "The poker on her poor head! Oh, sir, she's not dead, is she?"

"Not a bit. Come along, where's her room?" Reggie picked her up.

The man from the car was at his elbow. "Thank you, I'll do that," he said.

"Why, it's Mr. Woodcote. Fancy that!" Reggie smiled. "But why should the dramatist carry the leading lady?"

"I'm her husband," said Woodcote fiercely. "Any objection, Mr. Fortune?"

"Oh, no, Mr. Smith. I beg pardon, Mr. Woodcote. But you'll want me, you know. If it's only to sew her up."

He bore the lady off to her bedroom.

* * * * * *

The case ended as it began, with a morning voyage in a punt. Lomas brought that craft in to the landing-stage and embarked Reggie, who laid himself down on the cushions elaborately and sighed. "My dear fellow, I know you were always a lady's man," Lomas remonstrated. "But you're overdoing it. You're enfeebled. You wilt."

Reggie moaned gently. "I know it. I feel like a curate, Lomas. They coo over me. It's weakening to the intellect. Rose holds my hand and tells me she's sorry she was so naughty, and Sylvia looks tenderly from her unbandaged eye and says she'll never do it again."

"Have you got anything rational out of them?"

"I have it all. It's quite simple. Sylvia heard that Rose was trying to do her out of the part. She was pained. She went round in a hurry to talk to Rose. In the garden she saw Albert Edward, the chauffeur, who told her that Rose was on the boat-house balcony, her favourite place on a fine evening. Sylvia went there straight. Hence none of the servants but Albert Edward knew that Sylvia had called that night. Sylvia and Rose had words. Sylvia says she offered Rose quite a good minor part. Rose says Sylvia insulted her. I fear that Rose tried to slap her face. Anyway, Sylvia tumbled down the boat-house steps and there was a splash. Rose heard it and thought Sylvia had gone in and was delighted. Albert Edward heard it as he had heard the row, and thought something could be done about it. But he saw Sylvia rush off rather draggled round the skirts, and knew she wasn't drowned. Rose didn't take the trouble to see Sylvia scramble out. She was too happy. Sylvia was annoyed, but she has an ingenious mind. It occurred to her that if she did a disappearance Rose would get the wind up badly and it would be a howling advertisement for Miss Sylvia Sheridan and Woodcote's new play. Yes, Lomas dear, you were quite right. Only Bell was too. Sylvia scurried off to London and let herself into her flat and telephoned to Woodcote and told him all about it. He was badly gone on Sylvia before. He gave way to his emotions and those two geese arranged their elopement that night. She went off at break of day and he got a special licence. Meanwhile Albert Edward was getting busy. He collected the cigarette-case from the boat-house first thing in the morning, he found out Sylvia hadn't gone home and he started blackmailing Rose. That was why we saw her looking desperate. She got more and more funky, she paid that bright lad all the money she could spare (the clean notes) and most of her jewellery (the pawn-tickets). The only thing that worried Albert Edward was when Sylvia would turn up again. Hence that interest in the parlourmaid which gave him away. Poor Rose tried to drown her sorrows in morphia, and when she found Albert Edward was in the cells, she wanted to go under quiet and quick."

"I have a mild, manly longing to smack Sylvia," said Lomas.

"Well, well. The housekeeper did that. With a poker," Reggie murmured. "Life is quite just to the wicked. But wearing to the virtuous. I am much worn, Lomas. I want my lunch."

CASE VII

THE UNKNOWN MURDERER

ONCE upon a time a number of men in a club discussed how Mr. Reginald Fortune came to be the expert adviser of the Home Office upon crime. The doctors admitted that though he is a competent surgeon, pathologist and what not, he never showed international form. There was a Fellow of the Royal Society who urged that Fortune knew more about natural science than most schoolboys, politicians and civil servants. An artist said he had been told Fortune understood business, and his banker believed Fortune was a judge of old furniture. But they all agreed that he is a jolly good fellow. Which means, being interpreted, he can be all things to all men.

Mr. Fortune himself is convinced that he was meant by Providence to be a general practitioner: to attend to my lumbago and your daughter's measles. He has been heard to complain of the chance that has made him, knowing something of everything, nothing completely, into a specialist. His only qualification, he will tell you, is that he doesn't get muddled.

There you have it, then. He is singularly sensitive to people. "Very odd how he knows men," said Superintendent Bell reverently. "As if he had an extra sense to tell him of people's souls, like smells or colours." And he has a clear head. He is never confused about what is important and what isn't, and he has never been known to hesitate in doing what is necessary.

Consider his dealing with the affair of the unknown murderer.

There was not much interesting crime that Christmas. The singular case of Sir Humphrey Bigod, who was found dead in a chalkpit on the eve of his marriage, therefore obtained a lot of space in the papers, which kept it up, even after the coroner's jury had declared for death by misadventure, with irrelevant inventions and bloodthirsty hints of murder and tales of clues. This did not disturb the peace of the scientific adviser to the Criminal Investigation Department, who knew that the lad was killed by a fall and that there was no means of knowing any more. Mr. Fortune was much occupied in being happy, for after long endeavour he had engaged Joan Amber to marry him. The lady has said the endeavour was hers, but I am not now telling that story. Just after Christmas she took him to the children's party at the Home of Help.

It is an old-fashioned orphanage, a huge barrack of a building, but homely and kind. Time out of mind people of all sorts, with old titles and new, with money and with brains, have been the friends of its children. When Miss Amber brought Reggie Fortune under the flags and the strings of paper roses into its hall, which was as noisy as the parrot house, he gasped slightly. "Be brave, child," she said. "This is quiet to what it will be after tea. And cool. You will be much hotter. You don't know how hot you'll be."

"Woman, you have deceived me," said Mr. Fortune bitterly. "I thought philanthropists were respectable."

"Yes, dear. Don't be frightened. You're only a philanthropist for the afternoon."

"I ask you. Is that Crab Warnham?"

"Of course it's Captain Warnham." Miss Amber smiled beautifully at a gaunt man with a face like an old jockey. He flushed as he leered back. "Do you know his wife? She's rather precious."

"Poor woman. He doesn't look comfortable here, does he? The last time I saw Crab Warnham was in a place that's several kinds of hell in Berlin. He was quite at home there."

"Forget it," said Miss Amber gently. "You will when you meet his wife. And their boy's a darling."

"His boy?" Reggie was startled.

"Oh, no. She was a widow. He worships her and the child."

Reggie said nothing. It appeared to him that Captain Warnham, for a man who worshipped his wife, had a hungry eye on women. And the next moment Captain Warnham was called to attention. A small woman, still pretty though earnest, talked to him like a mother or a commanding officer. He was embarrassed, and when she had done with him he fled.

The small woman, who was austerely but daintily clad in black with some white at the neck, continued to flit among the company, finding everyone a job of work. "She says to one, Go, and he goeth, and to another, Come, and he cometh. And who is she, Joan?"

"Lady Chantry," said Miss Amber. "She's providence here, you know."

And Lady Chantry was upon them. Reggie found himself looking down into a pair of uncommonly bright eyes and wondering what it felt like to be as strenuous as the little woman who was congratulating him on Joan, thanking him for being there and arranging his afternoon for him all in one breath. He had never heard anyone talk so fast. In a condition of stupor he saw Joan reft from him to tell the story of Cinderella to magic lantern pictures in one dormitory, while he was led to another to help in a scratch concert. And as the door closed on him he heard the swift clear voice of Lady Chantry exhorting staff and visitors to play round games.

He suffered. People who had no voices sang showy songs, people who had too much voice sang ragtime to those solemn, respectful children. In pity for the children and himself he set up as a conjurer, and the dormitory was growing merry when a shriek cut into his patter. "That's only my bones creaking," he went on quickly, for the children were frightened; "they always do that when I put the knife in at the ear and take it out of my hind leg. So. But it doesn't hurt. As the motor-car said when it ran over the policeman's feet. All done by kindness. Come here, Jenny Wren. You mustn't use your nose as a money-box." A small person submitted to have pennies taken out of her face.

The door opened and a pallid nurse said faintly: "The doctor. Are you the doctor?"

"Of course," said Reggie. "One moment, people. Mr. Punch has fallen over the baby. It always hurts him. In the hump. Are we down-hearted? No. Pack up your troubles in the old kit bag ——" He went out to a joyful roar of that lyric. "What's the trouble?" The nurse was shaking.

"In there, sir-she's up there."

Reggie went up the stairs in quick time. The door of a little sitting-room stood open. Inside it people were staring at a woman who sat at her desk. Her dress was dark and wet. Her head lolled forward. A deep gash ran across her throat.

"Yes. There's too many of us here," he said, and waved the spectators away. One lingered, an old woman, large and imposing, and announced that she was the matron. Reggie shut the door and came back to the body in the chair. He held the limp hands a moment, he lifted the head and looked close into the flaccid face. "When was she found? When I heard that scream? Yes." He examined the floor. "Quite so." He turned to the matron. "Well, well. Who is she?"

"It's our resident medical officer, Dr. Emily Hall. But Dr. Fortune, can't you do anything?"

"She's gone," said Reggie.

"But this is terrible, doctor. What does it mean?"

"Well, I don't know what it means. Her throat was cut by a highly efficient knife, probably from behind. She lingered a little while quite helpless, and died. Not so very long ago. Who screamed?"

"The nurse who found her. One of our own girls, Dr. Fortune, Edith Baker. She was always a favourite of poor Dr. Hall's. She has been kept on here at Dr. Hall's wish to train as a nurse. She was devoted to Dr. Hall. One of these girlish passions."

"And she came into the room and found-this-and screamed?"

"So she tells me," said the matron.

"Well, well," Reggie sighed. "Poor kiddies! And now you must send for the police."

"I have given instructions, Dr. Fortune," said the matron with dignity.

"And I think you ought to keep Edith Baker from talking about it." Reggie opened the door.

"Edith will not talk," said the matron coldly. "She is a very reserved creature."

"Poor thing. But I'm afraid some of our visitors will. And they had better not, you know." At last he got rid of the lady and turned the key in the lock and stood looking at it. "Yes, quite natural, but very convenient," said he, and turned away from it and contemplated a big easy chair. The loose cushion on the seat showed that somebody had been sitting in it, a fact not in itself remarkable. But there was a tiny smear of blood on the arm still wet. He picked up the cushion. On the under side was a larger smear of blood. Mr. Fortune's brow contracted. "The unknown murderer cuts her throat-comes over here-makes a mess on the chair-turns the cushion over-and sits down-to watch the woman die. This is rather diabolical." He began to wander round the room. It offered him no other signs but some drops of blood on the hearthrug and the hearth. He knelt down and peered into the fire, and with the tongs drew from it a thin piece of metal. It was a surgical knife. He looked at the dead woman. "From your hospital equipment, Dr. Hall. And Edith Baker is a nurse. And Edith Baker had 'a girlish passion' for you. I wonder."

Some one was trying the door. He unlocked it, to find an inspector of police. "I am Reginald Fortune," he explained. "Here's your case."

"I've heard of you, sir," said the inspector reverently. "Bad business, isn't it? I'm sure it's very lucky you were here."

"I wonder," Reggie murmured.

"Could it be suicide, sir?"

Reggie shook his head. "I wish it could. Not a nice murder. Not at all a nice murder. By the way, there's the knife. I picked it out of the fire."

"Doctor's tool, isn't it, sir? Have you got any theory about it?" Reggie shook his head. "There's the girl who gave the alarm: she's a nurse in the hospital, I'm told."

"I don't know the girl," said Reggie. "You'd better see what you make of the room. I shall be downstairs."

In the big hall the decorations and the Christmas tree with its ungiven presents glowed to emptiness and silence. Joan Amber came forward to meet him. He did not speak to her. He continued to stare at the ungiven presents on the Christmas tree. "What do you want to do?" she said at last.

"This is the end of a perfect day," said Mr. Fortune. "Poor kiddies."

"The matron packed them all off to their dormitories."

Mr. Fortune laughed. "Just as well to rub it in, isn't it?"

Miss Amber did not answer him for a moment. "Do you know, you look rather terrible?" she said, and indeed his normally plump, fresh-coloured, cheery face had a certain ferocity.

"I feel like a fool, Joan. Where is everybody?"

"She sent everybody away too."

"She would. Great organizer. No brain. My only aunt! A woman's murdered and every stranger who was in the place is hustled off before the police get to work. This isn't a crime, it's a nightmare."

"Well, of course they were anxious to go."

"They would be."

"Reggie, who are you thinking of?"

"I can't think. There are no facts. Where's this matron now?"

The inspector came upon them as they were going to her room. "I've finished upstairs, sir. Not much for me, is there? Plenty downstairs, though. I reckon I'll hear some queer stories before I've done. These homes are always full of gossip. People living too close together, wonderful what bad blood it makes. I— —" He broke off and stared at Reggie. From the matron's room came the sound of sobbing. He opened the door without a knock.

The matron sat at her writing-table, coldly judicial. A girl in nurse's uniform was crying on the bosom of Lady Chantry, who caressed her and murmured in her ear.

"Sorry to interrupt, ma'am," the inspector said, staring hard.

"You don't interrupt. This girl is Edith Baker, who seems to have been the last person who saw Dr. Hall alive and was certainly the first person who saw her dead."

"And who was very, very fond of her," Lady Chantry said gently. "Weren't you, dear?"

"I'll have to take her statement," said the inspector. But the girl was torn with sobbing.

"Come, dear, come." Lady Chantry strove with her. "The Inspector only wants you to say how you left her and how you found her."

"Edith, you must control yourself." The matron lifted her voice.

"I hate you," the girl cried, and tore herself away and rushed out of the room.

"She'll have to speak, you know, ma'am," the inspector said.

"I am very sorry to say she has always had a passionate temperament," said the matron.

"Poor child!" Lady Chantry rose. "She was so fond of the doctor, you see. I'll go to her, matron, and see what I can do."

"Does anyone here know what the girl was up to this afternoon, ma'am?" said the inspector.

"I will try to find out for you," said the matron, and rang her bell.

"Well, well," said Reggie Fortune. "Every little helps. You might find out what all the other people were doing this afternoon."

The matron stared at him. "Surely you're not thinking of the visitors, Mr. Fortune?"

"I'm thinking of your children," said Reggie, and she was the more amazed. "Not a nice murder, you know, not at all a nice murder."

And then he took Miss Amber home. She found him taciturn, which is his habit when he is angry. But she had never seen him angry before. She is a wise woman. When he was leaving her: "Do you know what it is about you, sir?" she said. "You're always just right."

When the Hon. Sidney Lomas came to his room in Scotland Yard the next morning, Reggie Fortune was waiting for him. "My dear fellow!" he protested. "What is this? You're not really up, are you? It's not eleven. You're an hallucination."

"Zeal, all zeal, Lomas. The orphanage murder is my trouble."

"Have you come to give yourself up? I suspected you from the first, Fortune. Where is it?" He took a copy of the "Daily Wire" from the rack. "Yes. 'Dr. Reginald Fortune, the eminent surgeon, was attending the function and was able to give the police a first-hand account of the crime. Dr. Fortune states that the weapon used was a surgical knife.' My dear fellow, the case looks black indeed."

Reggie was not amused. "Yes. I also was present. And several others," he said. "Do you know anything about any of us?"

Lomas put up his eyeglass. "There's a certain bitterness about you, Fortune. This is unusual. What's the matter?"

"I don't like this murder," said Reggie. "It spoilt the children's party."

"That would be a by-product," Lomas agreed. "You're getting very domestic in your emotions. Oh, I like it, my dear fellow. But it makes you a little irrelevant."

"Domestic be damned. I'm highly relevant. It spoilt the children's party. Why did it happen at the children's party? Lots of other nice days to kill the resident medical officer."

"You're suggesting it was one of the visitors?"

"No, no. It isn't the only day visitors visit. I'm suggesting life is real, life is earnest-and rather diabolical sometimes."

"I'll call for the reports," Lomas said, and did so. "Good Gad! Reams! Barton's put in some heavy work."

"I thought he would," said Reggie, and went to read over Lomas's shoulder.

At the end Lomas lay back and looked up at him. "Well? Barton's put his money on this young nurse, Edith Baker."

"Yes. That's the matron's tip. I saw the matron. One of the world's organizers, Lomas. A place for everything and everything in its place. And if you don't fit, God help you. Edith Baker didn't fit. Edith Baker has emotions. Therefore she does murders. Q.E.D."

"Well, the matron ought to know the girl."

"She ought," Reggie agreed. "And our case is, gentlemen, that the matron who ought to know girls says Edith Baker isn't a nice young person. Lomas dear, why do policemen always believe what they're told? What the matron don't like isn't evidence."

"There is some evidence. The girl had one of these hysterical affections for the dead woman, passionately devoted and passionately jealous and so forth. The girl had access to the hospital instruments. All her time in the afternoon can't be accounted for, and she was the first to know of the murder."

"It's not good enough, Lomas. Why did she give the alarm?"

Lomas shrugged. "A murderer does now and then. Cunning or fright."

"And why did she wait for the children's party to do the murder?"

"Something may have happened there to rouse her jealousy."

"Something with one of the visitors?" Reggie suggested. "I wonder." And then he laughed. "A party of the visitors went round the hospital, Lomas. They had access to the surgical instruments."

"And were suddenly seized with a desire for homicide? They also went to the gymnasium and the kitchen. Did any of them start boiling potatoes? My dear Fortune, you are not as plausible as usual."

"It isn't plausible," Reggie said. "I know that. It's too dam' wicked."

"Abnormal," Lomas nodded. "Of course the essence of the thing is that it's abnormal. Every once in a while we have these murders in an orphanage or school or some place where women and children are herded together. Nine times out of ten they are cases of hysteria. Your young friend Miss Baker seems to be a highly hysterical subject."

"You know more than I do."

"Why, that's in the evidence. And you saw her yourself half crazy with emotion after the murder."

"Good Lord!" said Reggie. "Lomas, old thing, you do run on. Pantin' time toils after you in vain. That girl wasn't crazy. She was the most natural of us all. You send a girl in her teens into the room where the woman she is keen on is sitting with her throat cut. She won't talk to you like a little lady. The evidence! Why do you believe what people tell you about people? They're always lying—by accident if not on purpose. This matron don't like the girl because she worshipped the lady doctor. Therefore the girl is called abnormal and jealous. Did you never hear of a girl in her teens worshipping a teacher? It's common form. Did you never hear of another teacher being vicious about it? That's just as common."

"Do you mean the matron was jealous of them both?"

Reggie shrugged. "It hits you in the eye."

"Good Gad!" said Lomas. "Do you suspect the matron?"

"I suspect the devil," said Reggie gravely. "Lomas, my child, whoever did that murder cut the woman's throat and then sat down in her easy chair and watched her die. I call that devilish." And he told of the blood-stains and the turned cushions.

"Good Gad," said Lomas once more, "there's some hate in that."

"Not a nice murder. Also it stopped the children's party."

"You harp on that." Lomas looked at him curiously. "Are you thinking of the visitors?"

"I wonder," Reggie murmured. "I wonder."

"Here's the list," Lomas said, and Reggie came slowly to look. "Sir George and Lady Bean, Lady Chantry, Mrs. Carroway,"—he ran his pencil down—"all well-known, blameless busybodies, full of good works. Nothing doing."

"Crab Warnham," said Reggie.

"Oh, Warnham: his wife took him, I suppose. She's a saint, and he eats out of her hand, they say. Well, he was a loose fish, of course, but murder! I don't see Warnham at that."

"He has an eye for a woman."

"Still? I dare say. But good Gad, he can't have known this lady doctor. Was she pretty?" Reggie nodded. "Well, we might look for a link between them. Not likely, is it?"

"We're catching at straws," said Reggie sombrely.

Lomas pushed the papers away. "Confound it, it's another case without evidence. I suppose it can't be suicide like that Bigod affair?"

Reggie, who was lighting a cigar, looked up and let the match burn his fingers. "Not suicide. No," he said. "Was Bigod's?"

"Well, it was a deuced queer death by misadventure."

"As you say." Reggie nodded and wandered dreamily out.

This seems to have been the first time that anyone thought of comparing the Bigod case to the orphanage murder. When the inquest on the lady doctor was held the police had no more evidence to produce than you have heard, and the jury returned a verdict of murder by some person or persons unknown. Newspapers strove to enliven the dull calm of the holiday season by declaiming against the inefficiency of a police force which allowed murderers to remain anonymous, and hashed up the Bigod case again to prove that the fall of Sir Humphrey Bigod into his chalkpit, though called accidental, was just as mysterious as the cut throat of Dr. Hall. And the Hon. Sidney Lomas cursed the man who invented printing.

These assaults certainly did not disturb Reggie Fortune, who has never cared what people say of him. With the help of Joan Amber he found a quiet remote place for the unhappy girl suspected of the murder (Lady Chantry was prettily angry with Miss Amber about that, protesting that she wanted to look after Edith herself), and said he was only in the case as a philanthropist. After which he gave all his time to preparing his house and Miss Amber for married life. But the lady found him dreamy.

It was in fact while he was showing her how the new colours in the drawing-room looked under the new lighting that Dr. Eden called him up. Dr. Eden has a general practice in Kensington. Dr. Eden wanted to consult him about a case: most urgent: 3 King William's Walk.

"May I take the car?" said Reggie to Joan. "He sounds rattled. You can go on home afterwards. It's not far from you either. I wonder who lives at 3 King William's Walk."

"But it's Mrs. Warnham!" she cried.

"Oh, my aunt!" said Reggie Fortune; and said no more.

And Joan Amber could not call him out of his thoughts. She was as grave as he. Only when he was getting out of the car, "Be good to her, dear," she said gently. He kissed the hand on his arm.

The door was opened by a woman in evening-dress. "It is Mr. Fortune, isn't it? Please come in. It's so kind of you to come." She turned to the maid in the background. "Tell Dr. Eden, Maggie. It's my little boy—and we are so anxious."

"I'm very sorry, Mrs. Warnham." Reggie took her hand and found it cold. The face he remembered for its gentle calm was sternly set. "What is the trouble?"

"Gerald went to a party this afternoon. He came home gloriously happy and went to bed. He didn't go to sleep at once, he was rather excited, but he was quite well. Then he woke up crying with pain and was very sick. I sent for Dr. Eden. It isn't like Gerald to cry, Mr. Fortune. And— —"

A hoarse voice said "Catherine, you oughtn't to be out there in the cold." Reggie saw the gaunt face of Captain Warnham looking round a door at them.

"What does it matter?" she cried. "Dr. Eden doesn't want me to be with him, Mr. Fortune. He is still in pain. And I don't think Dr. Eden knows."

Dr. Eden came down in time to hear that. A large young man, he stood over them looking very awkward and uncomfortable.

"I'm sure Dr. Eden has done everything that can be done," said Reggie gently. "I'll go up, please." And they left the mother to her husband, that flushed, gaunt face peering round the corner as they kept step on the stairs.

"The child's seven years old," said Eden. "There's no history of any gastric trouble. Rather a good digestion. And then this—out of the blue!" Reggie went into a nursery where a small boy lay huddled and restless with all the apparatus of sickness by his bed. He raised a pale face on which beads of sweat stood.

"Hallo, Gerald," Reggie said quietly. "Mother sent me up to make you all right again." He took the child's hand and felt for the pulse. "I'm Mr. Fortune, your fortune, good fortune."

The child tried to smile and Reggie's hands moved over the uneasy body and all the while he murmured softly nonsense talk....

The child did not want him to go, but at last he went off with Eden into a corner of the room. "Quite right to send for me," he said gravely, and Eden put his hand to his head. "I know. I know. It's horrible when it's a child. One of the irritant poisons. Probably arsenic. Have you given an emetic?"

"He's been very sick. And he's so weak."

"I know. Have you got anything with you?"

"I sent home. But I didn't care to——"

"I'll do it. Sulphate of zinc. You go and send for a nurse. And find some safe milk. I wouldn't use the household stuff."

"My God, Fortune! Surely it was at the party?"

"Not the household stuff," Reggie repeated, and he went back to the child....

It was many hours afterwards that he came softly downstairs. In the hall husband and wife met him. It seemed to him that it was the man who had been crying. "Are you going away?" Mrs. Warnham said.

"There's no more pain. He is asleep."

Her eyes darkened. "You mean he's—dead?" the man gasped.

"I hope he'll live longer than any of us, Captain Warnham. But no one must disturb him. The nurse will be watching, you know. And I'm sure we all want to sleep sound-don't we?" He was gone. But he stayed a moment on the doorstep. He heard emotions within.

On the next afternoon Dr. Eden came into his laboratory at St. Saviour's. "One moment. One moment." Reggie was bent over a notebook. "When I go to hell they'll set me doing sums." He frowned at his figures. "The third time is lucky. That's plausible if it isn't right. Well, how's our large patient?"

"He's doing well. Quite easy and cheerful."

Reggie stood up. "I think we might say, thank God."

"Yes, rather. I thought he was gone last night, Fortune. He would have been without you. It was wonderful how he bucked up in your hands. You ought to have been a children's specialist."

"My dear chap! Oh, my dear chap! I'm the kind of fellow who would always ought to have been something else. And so I'm doing sums in a laboratory which God knows I'm not fit for."

"Have you found out what it was?"

"Oh, arsenic, of course. Quite a fair dose he must have had. It's queer how they always will use arsenic."

Eden stared at him. "What are we to do?" he said in a low voice. "Fortune, I suppose it couldn't have been accidental?"

"What is a child likely to eat in which he would find grains of accidental arsenic?"

"Yes, but then——I mean, who could want to kill that child?"

"That is the unknown quantity in the equation. But people do want to murder children, quite nice children."

Eden grew pale. "What do you mean? You know he's not Warnham's child. Warnham's his step-father."

"Yes. Yes. Have you ever seen the two together?"

Eden hesitated. "He-well, he didn't seem to take to Warnham. But I'd have sworn Warnham was fond of him."

"And that's all quite natural, isn't it? Well, well. I hope he's in."

"What do you mean to do?"

"Tell Mrs. Warnham-with her husband listening."

Dr. Eden followed him out like a man going to be hanged.

Mrs. Warnham indeed met them in her hall. "Mr. Fortune,"—she took his hand, she had won back her old calm, but her eyes grew dark as she looked at him—"Gerald has been asking for you. And I want to speak to you."

"I shall be glad to talk over the case with you and Captain Warnham," said Reggie gravely. "I'll see the small boy first, if you don't mind." And the small boy kept his Mr. Fortune a long time.

Mrs. Warnham had her husband with her when the doctors came down. "I say, Fortune," Captain Warnham started up, "awfully good of you to take so much trouble. I mean to say,"—he cleared his throat—"I feel it, you know. How is the little beggar?"

"There's no reason why he shouldn't do well," Reggie said slowly. "But it's a strange case. Captain Warnham. Yes, a strange case. You may take it, there is no doubt the child was poisoned."

"Poisoned!" Warnham cried out in that queer hoarse voice.

"You mean it was something Gerald shouldn't have eaten?" Mrs. Warnham said gently.

"It was arsenic, Captain Warnham. Not much more than an hour before the time he felt ill, perhaps less, he had swallowed enough arsenic to kill him."

"I say, are you certain of all that? I mean to say, no doubt about anything?" Warnham was flushed. "Arsenic-and the time-and the dose? It's pretty thick, you know."

"There is no doubt. I have found arsenic. I can estimate the dose. And arsenic acts within that time."

"But I can't believe it," Mrs. Warnham said. "It would be too horribly cruel. Mr. Fortune, couldn't it have been accident? Something in his food?"

"It was certainly in his food or drink. But not accident, Mrs. Warnham. That is not possible."

"I say, let's have it all out, Fortune," Warnham growled. "Do you suspect anyone?"

"That's rather for you, isn't it?" said Reggie.

"Who could want to poison Gerald?" Mrs. Warnham cried.

"He says some one did," Warnham growled.

"When do you suppose he took the stuff, Fortune? At the party or after he came home?"

"What did he have when he came home?"

Warnham looked at his wife. "Only a little milk. He wouldn't eat anything," she said. "And I tasted his milk, I remember. It was quite nice."

"That points to the party," Eden said.

"But I can't believe it. Who could want to poison Gerald?"

"I've seen some of the people who were there," Eden frowned. "I don't believe there's another child ill. Only this one of the whole party."

"Yes. Yes. A strange case," said Reggie. "Was there anyone there with a grudge against you, Mrs. Warnham?"

"I don't think there's anyone with a grudge against me in the world."

"I don't believe there is, Catherine," her husband looked at her. "But damn it. Fortune found the stuff in the child. I say, Fortune, what do you advise?"

"You're sure of your own household? There's nobody here jealous of the child?"

Mrs. Warnham looked her distress. "I couldn't, I couldn't doubt anybody. There isn't any reason. You know, it doesn't seem real."

"And there it is," Warnham growled.

"Yes. Well, I shouldn't talk about it, you know. When he's up again take him right away, somewhere quiet. You'll live with him yourself, of course. That's all safe. And I—well, I shan't forget the case. Good-bye."

"Oh, Mr. Fortune——" she started up and caught his hands.

"Yes, yes, good-bye," said Reggie, and got away. But as Warnham let them out he felt Warnham's lean hand grip into his arm.

"A little homely comfort would be grateful," Reggie murmured. "Come and have tea at the Academies, Eden. They keep a pleasing muffin." He sank down in his car at Eden's side with a happy sigh.

But Eden's brow was troubled. "Do you think the child will be safe now, Fortune?" he said.

"Oh, I think so. If it was Warnham or Mrs. Warnham who poisoned him——"

"Good Lord! You don't think that?"

"They are frightened," said Reggie placidly, "I frightened 'em quite a lot. And if it was somebody else-the child is going away and Mrs. Warnham will be eating and drinking everything he eats and drinks. The small Gerald will be all right. There remains only the little problem, who was it?"

"It's a diabolical affair. Who could want to kill that child?"

"Diabolical is the word," Reggie agreed. "And a little simple food is what we need," and they went into the club and through a long tea he talked to Eden of rock gardens and Chinese nursery rhymes.

But when Eden, somewhat dazed by his appetite and the variety of his conversation, was gone, he made for that corner of the club where Lomas sat drinking tea made in the Russian manner. He pointed a finger at the clear weak fluid. "It was sad and bad and mad and it was not even sweet," he complained. "Take care, Lomas. Think what's happened to Russia. You would never be happy as a Bolshevik."

"I understand that the detective police force is the one institution which has survived in Russia."

"Put down that repulsive concoction and come and take the air."

Lomas stared at him in horror. "Where's your young lady? I thought you were walking out. You're a faithless fellow, Fortune. Go and walk like a little gentleman." But there was that in Reggie's eye which made him get up with a groan. "You're the most ruthless man I know."

The car moved away from the club and Reggie shrank under his rug as the January east wind met them. "I hope you are cold," said Lomas. "What is it now?"

"It was nearly another anonymous murder," and Reggie told him the story.

"Diabolical," said Lomas.

"Yes, I believe in the devil," Reggie nodded.

"Who stood to gain by the child's death? It's clear enough. There's only Warnham. Mrs. Warnham was left a rich woman when her first husband died, old Staveleigh. Every one knew that was why Warnham was after her. But the bulk of the fortune would go to the child. So he took the necessary action. Good Gad! We all knew Crab Warnham didn't stick at a trifle. But this— —! Cold-blooded scoundrel. Can you make a case of it?"

"I like you, Lomas. You're so natural," Reggie said. "That's all quite clear. And it's all wrong. This case isn't natural, you see. It hath a devil."

"Do you mean to say it wasn't Warnham?"

"It wasn't Warnham. I tried to frighten him. He was frightened. But not for himself. Because the child has an enemy and he doesn't know who it is."

"Oh, my dear fellow! He's not a murderer because you like his face."

"Who could like his face? No. The poison was given at the party where Warnham wasn't."

"But why? What possible motive? Some homicidal lunatic goes to a Kensington children's party and picks out this one child to poison. Not very credible, is it?"

"No, it's diabolical. I didn't say a lunatic. When you tell me what lunacy is, we'll discuss whether the poisoner was sane. But the diabolical is getting a little too common, Lomas. There was Bigod: young, healthy, well off, just engaged to a jolly girl. He falls into a chalkpit and the jury says it was misadventure. There was the lady doctor: young, clean living, not a ghost of a past, everybody liking her. She is murdered and a girl who was very fond of her nearly goes mad over it. Now there's the small Gerald: a dear kid, his mother worships him, his step-father's mighty keen on him, everybody likes him. Somebody tries to poison him and nearly brings it off."

"What are you arguing, Fortune? It's odd the cases should follow one another. It's deuced awkward we can't clean them up. But what then? They're not really related. The people are unconnected. There's a different method of murder-if the Bigod case was murder. The only common feature is that the man who attempted murder is not known."

"You think so? Well, well. What I want to know is, was there any one at Mrs. Lawley's party in Kensington who was also at the Home of Help party and also staying somewhere near the chalkpit when Bigod fell into it. Put your men on to that."

"Good Gad!" said Lomas. "But the cases are not comparable-not in the same class. Different method-different kind of victim. What motive could any creature have for picking out just these three to kill?"

Reggie looked at him. "Not nice murders, are they?" he said. "I could guess-and I dare say we'll only guess in the end."

That night he was taking Miss Amber, poor girl, to a state dinner of his relations. They had ten minutes together before the horrors of the ceremony began and she was benign to him about the recovery of the small Gerald. "It was dear of you to ring up and tell me. I love Gerry. Poor Mrs. Warnham! I just had to go round to her and she was sweet. But she has been frightened. You're rather a wonderful person, sir. I didn't know you were a children's doctor-as well as a million other things. What was the matter? Mrs. Warnham didn't tell us. It must ——"

"Who are 'us,' Joan?"

"Why, Lady Chantry was with her. She didn't tell us what it really was. After we came away Lady Chantry asked me if I knew."

"But I'm afraid you don't," Reggie said. "Joan, I don't want you to talk about the small Gerry? Do you mind?"

"My dear, of course not." Her eyes grew bigger. "But Reggie-the boy's going to be all right."

"Yes. Yes. You're rather a dear, you know."

And at the dinner-table which then received them his family found him of an unwonted solemnity. It was agreed, with surprise and reluctance, that engagement had improved him: that there might be some merit in Miss Amber after all.

A week went by. He had been separated from Miss Amber for one long afternoon to give evidence in the case of the illegitimate Pekinese when she rang him up on the telephone. Lady Chantry, she said, had asked her to choose a day and bring Mr. Fortune to dine. Lady Chantry did so want to know him.

"Does she, though?" said Mr. Fortune.

"She was so nice about it," said the telephone. "And she really is a good sort, Reggie. She's always doing something kind."

"Joan," said Mr. Fortune, "you're not to go into her house."

"Reggie!" said the telephone.

"That's that," said Mr. Fortune. "I'll speak to Lady Chantry."

Lady Chantry was at home. She sat in her austerely pleasant drawing-room, toasting a foot at the fire, a small foot which brought out a pretty leg. Of course she was in black with some white about her neck, but the loose gown had grace. She smiled at him and tossed back her hair. Not a thread of white showed in its crisp brown and it occurred to Reggie that he had never seen a woman of her age carry off bobbed hair so well. What was her age? Her eyes were as bright as a bird's and her clear pallor was unfurrowed.

"So good of you, Mr. Fortune ——"

"Miss Amber has just told me ——"

They spoke together. She got the lead then. "It was kind of her to let you know at once. But she's always kind, isn't she? I did so want you to come, and make friends with me before you're married, and it will be very soon now, won't it? Oh, but do let me give you some tea."

"No tea, thank you."

"Won't you? Well, please ring the bell. I don't know how men can exist without tea. But most of them don't now, do they? You're almost unique, you know. I suppose it's the penalty of greatness."

"I came round to say that Miss Amber won't be able to dine with you, Lady Chantry."

It was a moment before she answered. "But that is too bad. She told me she was sure you could find a day."

"She can't come," said Reggie sharply.

"The man has spoken," she laughed. "Oh, of course, she mustn't go behind that." He was given a keen mocking glance. "And can't you come either, Mr. Fortune?"

"I have a great deal of work, Lady Chantry. It's come rather unexpectedly."

"Indeed, you do look worried. I'm so sorry. I'm sure you ought to take a rest, a long rest." A servant came in. "Won't you really have some tea?"

"No, thank you. Goodbye, Lady Chantry."

He went home and rang up Lomas. Lomas, like the father of Baby Bunting, had gone a-hunting. Lomas was in Leicestershire. Superintendent Bell replied: Did Bell know if they had anything new about the unknown murderer?

"Inquiries are proceeding, sir," said Superintendent Bell.

"Damn it, Bell, I'm not the House of Commons. Have you got anything?"

"Not what you'd call definite, sir, no."

"You'll say that on the Day of Judgment," said Reggie.

It was on the next day that he found a telegram waiting for him when he came home to dress for dinner:

Gerald ill again very anxious beg you will come sending car to meet evening trains.

Warnham

Fernhurst

Blackover.

He scrambled into the last carriage of the half-past six as it drew out of Waterloo.

Mrs. Warnham had faithfully obeyed his orders to take Gerald to a quiet place. Blackover stands an equally uncomfortable distance from two main lines, one of which throws out towards it a feeble and spasmodic branch. After two changes Reggie arrived, cold and with a railway sandwich rattling in his emptiness, on the dimly-lit platform of Blackover. The porter of all work who took his ticket thought there was a car outside.

In the dark station yard Reggie found only one: "Do you come from Fernhurst?" he called, and the small chauffeur who was half inside the bonnet shut it up and touched his cap and ran round to his seat.

They dashed off into the night, climbing up by narrow winding roads through woodland. Nothing passed them, no house gave a gleam of light. The car stopped on the crest of a hill and Reggie looked out. He could see nothing but white frost and pines. The chauffeur was getting down.

"What's the trouble?" said Reggie, with his head out of window: and slipped the catch and came out in a bundle.

The chauffeur's face was the face of Lady Chantry. He saw it in the flash of a pistol overhead as he closed with her. "I will, I will," she muttered, and fought him fiercely. Another shot went into the pines. He wrenched her hand round. The third was fired into her face. The struggling body fell away from him, limp.

He carried it into the rays of the headlights and looked close. "That's that," he said with a shrug, and put it into the car.

He lit a cigar and listened. There was no sound anywhere but the sough of the wind in the pines. He climbed into the chauffeur's place and drove away. At the next crossroads he took that which led north and west, and so in a while came out on the Portsmouth road.

That night the frost gathered on a motor-car in a lane between Hindhead and Shottermill. Mr. Fortune unobtrusively caught the last train from Haslemere.

When he came out from a matinee with Joan Amber next day, the newsboys were shouting "Motor Car Mystery." Mr. Fortune did not buy a paper.

It was on the morning of the second day that Scotland Yard sent for him. Lomas was with Superintendent Bell. The two of them received him with solemnity and curious eyes. Mr. Fortune was not pleased. "Dear me, Lomas, can't you keep the peace for a week at a time?" he protested. "What is the reason for your existence?"

"I had all that for breakfast," said Lomas. "Don't talk like the newspapers. Be original."

" 'Another Mysterious Murder,' " Reggie murmured, quoting headlines. " 'Scotland Yard Baffled Again,' 'Police Mandarins.' No, you haven't a 'good Press,' Lomas old thing."

Lomas said something about the Press. "Do you know who that woman chauffeur was, Fortune?"

"That wasn't in the papers, was it?"

"You haven't guessed?"

Again Reggie Fortune was aware of the grave curiosity in their eyes. "Another of our mysterious murders," he said dreamily. "I wonder. Are you working out the series at last? I told you to look for some one who was always present."

Lomas looked at Superintendent Bell. "Lady Chantry was present at this one, Fortune," he said. "Lady Chantry took out her car the day before yesterday. Yesterday morning the car was found in a lane above Haslemere. Lady Chantry was inside. She wore chauffeur's uniform. She was shot through the head."

"Well, well," said Reggie Fortune.

"I want you to come down and look at the body."

"Is the body the only evidence?"

"We know where she bought the coat and cap. Her own coat and hat were under the front seat. She told her servants she might not be back at night. No one knows what she went out for or where she went."

"Yes. Yes. When a person is shot, it's generally with a gun. Have you found it?"

"She had an automatic pistol in her hand."

Reggie Fortune rose. "I had better see her," he said sadly. "A wearing world, Lomas. Come on. My car's outside."

Two hours later he stood looking down at the slight body and the scorched wound in that pale face while a police surgeon demonstrated to him how the shot was fired. The pistol was gripped with the rigour of death in the woman's right hand, the bullet that was taken from the base of the skull fitted it, the muzzle-remark the stained, scorched flesh-must have been held close to her face when the shot was fired. And Reggie listened and nodded. "Yes, yes. All very clear, isn't it? A straight case." He drew the sheet over the body and paid compliments to the doctor as they went out.

Lomas was in a hurry to meet them. Reggie shook his head. "There's nothing for me, Lomas. And nothing for you. The medical evidence is suicide. Scotland Yard is acquitted without a stain on its character."

"No sort of doubt?" said Lomas.

"You can bring all the College of Surgeons to see her. You'll get nothing else."

And so they climbed into the car again. "Finis, thank God!" said Mr. Fortune as the little town ran by.

Lomas looked at him curiously. "Why did she commit suicide, Fortune?" he said.

"There are also other little questions," Reggie murmured. "Why did she murder Bigod? Why did she murder the lady doctor? Why did she try to murder the child?"

Lomas continued to stare at him. "How do you know she did?" he said in a low voice. "You're making very sure."

"Great heavens! You might do some of the work. I know Scotland Yard isn't brilliant, but it might take pains. Who was present at all the murders? Who was the constant force? Haven't you found that out yet?"

"She was staying near Bigod's place. She was at the orphanage. She was at the child's party. And only she was at all three. It staggered me when I got the evidence complete. But what in heaven makes you think she is the murderer?"

Reggie moved uneasily. "There was something malign about her."

"Malign! But she was always doing philanthropic work."

"Yes. It may be a saint who does that-or the other thing. Haven't you ever noticed-some of the people who are always busy about distress-they rather like watching distress?"

"Why, yes. But murder! And what possible motive is there for killing these different people? She might have hated one or another. But not all three."

"Oh, there is a common factor. Don't you see? Each one had somebody to feel the death like torture-the girl Bigod was engaged to, the girl who was devoted to the lady doctor, the small Gerald's mother. There was always somebody to suffer horribly-and the person to be killed was always somebody who had a young good life to lose. Not at all nice murders, Lomas. Genus diabolical, species feminine. Say that Lady Chantry had a devilish passion for cruelty-and it ended that night in the motor-car."

"But why commit suicide? Do you mean she was mad?"

"I wouldn't say that. That's for the Day of Judgment. When is cruelty madness? I don't know. Why did she-give herself away-in the end? Perhaps she found she had gone a little too far. Perhaps she knew you and I had begun to look after her. She never liked me much, I fancy. She was a little-odd-with me."

"You're an uncanny fellow, Fortune."

"My dear chap! Oh, my dear chap! I'm wholly normal. I'm the natural man," said Reggie Fortune.

www.ingramcontent.com/pod-product-compliance
Lightning Source LLC
LaVergne TN
LVHW021426300125
802476LV00002B/478